Further Scientific Mayhem with the Sugimori Sisters

Brigid Collins

Frosty Owl Publishing

Further Scientific Mayhem! with the Sugimori Sisters

Cover design © 2025 Brigid Collins

Frosty Owl Publishing

Paperback:
ISBN: 979-8-89728-019-3

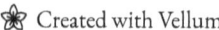 Created with Vellum

OTHER BOOKS BY BRIGID COLLINS

~

THE SONGBIRD RIVER CHRONICLES SERIES
Singer
The Southern Dragon
The Fount of Magic
The Dark Ways

WINTER'S CONSORT
A Prisoner to Spring
An Ally in Summer
An Enemy by Autumn
A Protector over Winter

THE CLOCKWORK KINGDOM SAGA
Clockwork Princess

FAIRIES AND FASTBALLS (With Ron Collins)
Home Run Enchanted
Curveball Cursed
Outfield Magicked

THE SUGIMORI SISTERS SERIES
The Scientific Adventures of the Sugimori Sisters
Further Scientific Mayhem! With the Sugimori Sisters
The Holiday Experiment Files of the Sugimori Sisters

NOVELLAS
Thorn and Thimble

SHORT FICTION
Three Tales of Faeries
Three Tales of Powers
Three Tales of Monsters
Three Tales of Nightmares

Acknowledgments

Thank you to my father for being my guinea pig on these stories, and to my mother for making them shine with perfect grammar and punctuation. Any remaining errors are my own.

Thank you to my friends Michael, Rob, Alex, and Clarence for all the lunches spent talking and commiserating about the business of writing.

ONE

The Unscheduled Extracurricular Detour

A crash of something heavy and metallic hitting the floor broke Ellen Sugimori out of her mental schedule shuffling. She paused halfway up the staircase and cocked her head to listen. As she suspected, the crash was followed by a string of frustrated exclamations, muffled by the door of the bedroom Ellen shared with her little sister, Risako, who fancied herself a scientist.

More like Mad Scientist, Ellen thought fondly as a wisp of gray smoke curled out from under the closed door. It smelled faintly like burning eggs.

But *eggs* reminded Ellen of the fact she'd skipped lunch in order to finish her geography homework today. She wouldn't have time to work on it later if she wanted to attend chess club this afternoon. Which started in an hour, she remembered.

It was a good thing Ellen was so used to Risako's scientific mishaps. She didn't have to waste time working up her nerves to open the bedroom door and see what sort of mess—mechanical, chemical, or supernatural—awaited her. She barely had time to come into their room at all right now, but the loss of her allotted half hour for piano practice would be worth it so long as Risako had something that could solve her scheduling problem.

She pushed the door open, and a cloud of egg-scented smoke blew in her face.

"I hope you're not too busy, Little Sister," she said, waving the smoke away.

Risako straightened from where she'd been crouching beside a large metal thing that lay between their two beds and ran a gloved hand through her already messy hair. Her white lab coat was streaked with soot to the point of becoming gray, but the look of frustration she wore was turning more thoughtful by the moment. "I'm extremely busy. I think metal will be more effective for my next prototype than cardboard, but I've never worked with it before. It's not cooperating. But maybe if I…"

She stroked her chin and crouched again.

Ellen cleared her throat. "I need your help with something."

"We can clean our room once I'm done with the experiment," Risako said without looking up. Her attention was riveted on the hunk of metal and the array of tools in an open toolbox beside her.

A twinge of alarm tingled through Ellen at the sight of the toolbox, and she snapped into Responsible Big Sister mode. Wasn't that Dad's? Those were real tools, not the strange cardboard contraptions Risako usually came up with. What did Little Sister think she was doing?

But Ellen wouldn't be able to ask unless she pried Risako's attention away from her machine. If she'd learned one thing from all the weird adventures these experiments sent them on, it was Risako's single-mindedness when it came to science. That, and the fact that Ellen even *had* a Responsible Big Sister mode.

In a louder voice, she said, "I need your help with something *scientific*."

Risako's head snapped up, and she was on her feet in a blink. "Ellen, you're doing science? That's *wonderful*. Tell me all about your hypothesis. Do you have test methods in mind?"

"Well, it's less that I'm *doing* science and more I have a problem I think science can solve. Your kind of science, to be exact."

"My kind of science, huh? What did you have in mind?"

Carefully, so as not to waste time explaining and re-explaining herself, Ellen laid out her problem. "The kids from my Japanese School class are starting an anime club, and I really want to join because one of the new kids brought his copy of the *Neko Hime* anime when his family moved here. They meet every Thursday at 4:00 in the school cafeteria, but my piano lesson with Mrs. Redford is also on Thursdays, and it wraps up at 3:45. I can't get from Mrs. Redford's house back to school in only fifteen minutes, not to mention getting back home after anime club ends so I don't miss dinner, so I need a way to cut out the travel time. I was hoping you'd worked on your time machine since, uh, *the last time*."

Ellen wouldn't ever forget their first misadventure with Little Sister's time machine prototype. Slogging through a prehistoric swamp and fighting off a hungry T. rex were the kinds of experiences that stuck with you. But the chance to see the new *Neko Hime* anime before it hit the streaming services here in America and then get to talk about it with other anime fans? That was worth pulling out the prototype again. Besides, Little Sister had been working on it now and then. Surely she'd worked out most of the kinks by now.

But Risako was already shaking her head by the time Ellen

finished. "No, no, you don't want the time machine for this. The time jump you're asking for is too small for the coordinate-sensors to work with, even with my recent calibrations."

Ellen's shoulders slumped. "So, you can't help me?"

"I didn't say that," Risako said. "No, what you need is a teleporter. Something that can zap you from one location to another with the press of a button!"

Risako moved over to the closet the two of them shared and flung the doors open. She had a wild gleam in her eyes now, one that Ellen recognized quite easily. The idea had taken hold of Risako, and she'd pursue it like a wolf on a rabbit until she got results. She was always single-minded like that. Ellen envied her, sometimes.

"You have one of those?" Ellen asked while checking her watch. She was making good time here. Securing Risako's help and getting her attention away from the box of Dad's tools in less than three minutes? Maybe she was starting to get the hang of this time-management thing.

"Not exactly, but I've got the pieces here and there from old experiments. They didn't work out for what I originally intended, but now that you've given me the inspiration for a teleporter, I think I can make them play nice together for a solid prototype."

Her voice was muffled by the clutter of the closet. They'd shoved so much stuff into the tiny space it was a wonder Little Sister ever found any of her old experiments. But sooner than Ellen expected, Little Sister emerged from the mess with a triumphant laugh.

"These should do the trick," she said, and carried her armload of—what looked to Ellen like—junk over to her work-table. She dumped the items over the empty surface with a rustle of cardboard, pipe cleaners, and construction paper, a clatter of plastic bottle caps and short lengths of hose, and a tiny tinkling sound of what looked suspiciously like some of Mom's sewing pins.

"Uh," said Ellen, "What's with all this stuff from Mom and Dad's... never mind."

She didn't have time to divert their attention to what sure looked like misbehavior on Little Sister's part. Once her scheduling problem was solved, she would have all the time in the world to either look into Risako's other projects or tell Mom and Dad about it herself.

Besides, Mom and Dad would surely notice their things were missing on their own.

Satisfied that her duties as Responsible Big Sister were finished, Ellen emerged from her worries to see that Risako had already pieced a few things together. What she had spread on the table before her now was a mix between a folded paper hat and a propeller beanie.

"There! Try that on," Little Sister said, thrusting the strange headwear at Ellen.

Skeptical, Ellen took the hat. She reminded herself that anything was worth getting to join anime club without dropping her other extracurriculars, even looking ridiculous.

She put the hat on.

A strange tingle ran over the top of her head, but once it faded away, nothing else happened.

"What am I supposed to do?" Ellen asked, feeling even stupider than usual around Little Sister.

Little Sister reached up and adjusted the way the hat sat on Ellen's head, then grabbed Ellen's hand as if they were about to cross a street together. "Okay, I'm pretty sure you've got it on correctly now. All you gotta do is think about where you want to go."

Ellen figured she'd better pick somewhere close by, just in case anything went wacky. Carefully, she pictured their backyard, making sure she got the arrangement of the house, the garage, and the lawn all properly placed in her mental image. For extra concentration, she closed her eyes.

The tingle washed over her again, stronger this time. A sudden sense of movement yanked from somewhere around her tummy, and she stumbled a little against losing her balance.

She opened her eyes to find herself standing in the backyard, precisely where she'd imagined. Little Sister stood beside her, still holding her hand, and beaming with success.

"It worked! Here, take us back up to our room so I can make some notes. Such a successful first test needs to be documented."

Risako tugged on Ellen's hand in emphasis.

"Okay, okay. Stop pulling," Ellen said, closing her eyes again. She imagined their bedroom, making sure to get the piles of junk spilling from the closet right, as well as the strange metal prototype in the middle of the floor.

The tingling came, then the sense of movement. Ellen was ready for it this time, so she didn't stumble.

They appeared just where Ellen wanted them to. Well, maybe a little to the left, but it was so close the difference didn't matter.

Little Sister dropped Ellen's hand and skipped over to her table. She swept a notebook and pencil up and turned to face Ellen. The light of scientific discovery blazed in her eyes now, and Ellen took a tiny step backwards.

Even working on a project Ellen had requested, Risako could be a little too intense.

"Tell me everything you experienced when we jumped," Risako said, pencil hovering over a blank notebook page. "If you confirm my hypothesis, we might be looking at a break-through, not only on this new teleporter, but on my other project, too!"

But Ellen glanced at her watch. Their experimentation had taken up a lot more time than she'd thought. Chess club started in ten minutes, which wasn't anywhere near enough time to get back to school, even riding her bike.

Luckily, this prototype didn't seem to display any of the unpredictability of Risako's other machines.

"Sorry, Little Sister. I've got to get to chess club now. I'll help you with your experiments more later, okay? I'll tell you all about my trip to chess club and back after dinner tonight."

She'd slot it in somewhere between the hour she needed for finishing her math homework and the half hour allotted to taking a bath. It shouldn't be too hard, now that she had a teleporter blowing her schedule wide open. In fact, she'd probably discover all kinds of unused time she could put to work getting things done and joining more clubs!

Risako frowned and lowered the notebook. "Can't we at least write down your preliminary observations? We could do a lot with just that: make the ride smoother, zero in the calibration, apply some shock absorption—"

"Sure, definitely," Ellen said, her mind already focused on envisioning the classroom where chess club was held. The chalkboard would be wiped clean, the desks arranged in rows rather than the pairs they used when playing chess, the window blinds all pulled down to block the late afternoon sun. "We'll do all that when I get back. Gotta go!"

Closing her eyes, Ellen triggered the tingling sensation.

She missed Little Sister's look of disappointment.

She stumbled on arrival again, but only because she'd somehow wound up landing in the supply closet across the hall from the classroom. Her travel time *had* been accompanied by a definite sideways pull. Apparently, the teleporter hat wanted to list to the left. That was okay, so long as it dropped her close enough to her destination that her travel time was still saved.

Luckily, she avoided knocking anything over in the tight space of the closet and opened the door to step out before any of the other club members came. She took the teleporter hat off, folded it carefully, and put it in her pocket for safe keeping during the club meeting.

The meeting ended up being one of Ellen's best ones yet. Without the need to plan her timing to get home running through the back of her brain, she was better able to focus on her games, and she managed to take far more pieces than she normally did.

Feeling very accomplished, Ellen decided to stay late this time, helping to pack away the chess sets and rearrange the desks before saying good night to everyone as they all stepped out of the school building together, then went their separate ways.

Once she was alone on the sidewalk, Ellen pulled the teleporter hat back out of her pocket. It was a little creased, but she smoothed those lines away before setting it back on her head.

"Okay. Time to appear right in my usual chair for dinner," she said. Accounting for the teleporter's tendency to go farther left, she pictured the space to the right of her chair at the dinner table.

When she had the image firm in her mind, she closed her eyes.

Tingles raced across her head. The sensation of motion came, sharper than in the previous jumps, and the pull to the left was too obvious to ignore. To her horror, Ellen found herself *hurtling* to the left, and definitely *not* in the direction of home!

"Wait, stop, hold on!" she cried.

But the hat did not wait, stop, or hold on. It kept going to the left, faster and faster.

Ellen didn't dare open her eyes, afraid the motion would make her sick. She also didn't dare take the hat off, not until it finally came to a stop somewhere.

Oh, man, I should have let Little Sister do more tests, she thought. But it was too late now.

Finally, just when Ellen thought the hat might *never* stop, it did.

Ellen stumbled harder than any other landing and fell flat on her face into a pile of fine gray dust. The moment she sat up, sputtering dust out of her mouth, she snatched the teleporter off her head. She didn't want to risk a stray thought of home sending her on another who-knows-how-long journey. Besides, she had a headache now, and it was so cold her teeth were chattering.

Rubbing her arms, Ellen squinted through the pain in her head and looked around.

Gray dust as far as the eye could see, mostly flat, but occasionally broken by ring-shaped piles of dust—craters, Ellen realized. And the sky was full black, without a single cloud covering the twinkling stars. Ellen gaped up at them for a while, amazed. She'd never been anywhere with such a clear view of the night sky!

Then, she turned slightly, and a large, blue object came into her field of view. White and brown swirled with the blue to make it look rather like a marble.

Ellen lost her sense of amazement as fear took hold. That marble was *Earth*, any grade-schooler would recognize that blue marble image, and that meant—

She'd teleported herself all the way to the Moon!

≈

Luckily, Ellen was used enough to strange adventures that she got a handle on her panic before it could run away with her. Once she forced herself to slow her racing thoughts and take a deep breath, she realized that she *was* breathing. That meant there was plenty of air, despite the fact that the Moon wasn't supposed to have an atmosphere.

Curious, she looked at her surroundings again. The clear view of the night sky did show a little bit of a shimmer like light reflecting off a window, and it immediately reminded her of drawings she'd seen of big glass domes on places like the Moon or Mars, domes that held buildings or places for plants to grow.

She assumed she'd misremembered her science lessons on the Moon landings, because she didn't recall hearing that the old astronauts had built domes on the Moon. But they must have because she was clearly inside one of those kinds of domes now, one full of breathable oxygen.

And if that was the case, that must mean she'd find other stuff inside here with her.

"Well, no lesson like a hands-on lesson, I guess," she said. Brushing Moon-dust off her school clothes, Ellen started off in the direction that kept the blue marble of Earth in front of her.

The astronauts had left all kinds of machinery up here when they came back home. All Ellen had to do was to find those machines and figure out how to get a message back to Earth. Hopefully NASA would know how to get her in touch with Little Sister.

The walking warmed her up a little, but the cold still sank into her arms and legs. By the time she'd passed three small craters, her muscles were stiff with the Moon-chill. Still, she pressed on.

At least there were no T. rexes chasing her this time.

But she was really starting to get hungry, and even after walking past a few more craters, she hadn't found any sign of astronaut machines. By now, dinnertime had come and gone, and her stomach was growling loudly. She was frustrated with the lack of progress and the waste of time.

"What good is a teleporter if it takes more time to get where you're going than just going there at normal speed?" she grumped. She kicked at a Moon rock and scowled after it as it tumbled down a bank of gray dust.

The worst part was, she couldn't get her brain to stop shuffling and re-shuffling her schedule and focus on paying attention to her surroundings. She needed to keep an eye out for anything she could use to get a message back home, not worry about when she was gonna get her math homework done!

If she couldn't get home, she wouldn't need to do math homework tonight. Maybe not even this week.

Maybe not ever again.

Tears burned in her eyes, and she blinked furiously. She had never, *ever* wished more desperately to be sitting at the kitchen table, doing math homework!

A muffled squeak filled the Moon silence, and Ellen slapped a hand across her mouth to stifle any more sobs.

But the squeak came again, not from Ellen, but from somewhere to her right.

Ellen looked, and when she saw the little gray boy standing partially behind a Moon boulder and staring right at her with his big, egg-shaped black eyes, her mouth fell open.

He was dressed in a pair of silvery overalls and a hat woven from pink straw, and a metal bucket full of reddish leaves sat in the Moon dust beside him. All he lacked to look exactly like an alien farmer was a piece of grass sticking out of his mouth and a suntan.

The boy squeaked again, as he had done the first two times, and this time Ellen heard the note of question in the sound.

Gulping past the last of her tears, Ellen held out one hand. "I'm Ellen, and I'm lost. Can... can you help me?"

The alien boy tilted his head. "Elllln? Hepp?"

Ellen pointed up at the sky, at the blue marble in the sea of stars. "I have to get back to Earth."

"Rrrf."

"Yes, that's right," Ellen said, nodding. "Help?"

The boy stared at Earth, his huge black eyes unblinking, for a long time. Ellen tried to smother the antsy anxiety clamoring about wasted time.

Finally, the boy looked back at her and bobbed his gray head. "Hepp."

Beckoning with one long-fingered gray hand, the alien boy first bent to pick up his bucket of red leaves, then turned to walk behind the boulder.

Ellen didn't hesitate to follow him.

They passed the boulder and crested the outer lip of a large crater, the sides of which were quite tall. Tall enough to hide a full farm within it. Ellen gasped when the fields of red, blue, and purple plants came into view. The colors weren't vibrant, but more muted and dusty, as if the plants had drawn too much of the Moon dust up their stalks.

A pair of buildings were nestled down among the orderly rows, a little more round and pod-like than Ellen was used to seeing, but still clearly a farmhouse and a barn. The round, white barn stood open, and a cacophony of animal hoots and honks came from it. The farmhouse looked a little like an hourglass on its side, and each bulb of it trailed a tiny wisp of smoke from a thin chimney at the top.

Ellen sucked in a breath. Something smelled *delicious*.

By the time she'd stumbled down the slope of the crater and followed her farmer guide into the lane between the red and blue crops, the rest of the farmstead knew of her presence. A group of five similarly dressed gray alien folk met them at the house's half-circle porch, looking curious, but friendly. Three were of a similar size as the boy who'd brought her here, so Ellen assumed they were the farmers' kids.

One of them, an older man—judging by the wrinkles on his gray forehead—who had emerged from the house wearing a pink apron over his clothes and powder blue mitts on his hands, made an inquiring sound at the boy leading Ellen.

"Ellln," said the boy, gesturing at her. "Rrrf. Hepp."

"Hepp," said the man.

"Hepp," said another, a woman who had come from the barn. She scraped her dirty boots in the Moon dust and smiled at Ellen.

Ellen smiled back, feeling uncomfortable. "Uh, yes. Hepp. Thank you."

Then, to her utter embarrassment, her stomach let out the loudest growl she'd ever heard.

The older man clucked at her just like a mother chicken and stepped closer, arms out. He nodded at the house, and the four kids scampered inside while he waved at Ellen to follow.

The delicious smell got stronger inside, and Ellen almost moaned as she allowed the alien man to show her into a chair at their kitchen table.

She had no idea what any of this Moon food was called, but it was farm fresh and all tasty as she shoveled it into her mouth as fast as she could politely manage. There were multicolored veggies sauteed with some kind of poultry, warm rolls of a bread so soft it melted like a cloud in her mouth, and what turned out to be pink and orange eggs fried in a purple, sweet-tasting butter.

Once she'd eaten enough to quiet her rumbling stomach, she slowed down some. That's when she noticed how she was the only one at the table eating so single-mindedly. Everyone else alternated taking bites of their food with working on something in their hands. The older man knitted a mass of pink yarn, the woman tapped with a small hammer at a broken tool, and the boy who'd brought her here sorted out the contents of his bucket into separate crates at his feet. The other children had tasks, too.

The family all spoke to one another, but Ellen's observation soon revealed the absent-minded way the conversation was carried on.

And as soon as there were plates to clean, that task got added into the mix, as well. Ellen had never seen someone try to wash dishes and knit a sweater at the same time, but the alien man did.

"Wow, you guys seem really busy," she said.

Beside her, the boy who had led her here let out a very quiet sigh.

The alien woman, however, nodded with a pleased smile on her face. "Bzzzee."

Over at the sink, a sound of frustration joined with the splashing water and clicking knitting needles. Ellen glanced over to see the man struggling to accomplish both of his tasks. All he managed to do was to soak his knitting in dirty water, though.

Oblivious, the woman pushed something into Ellen's hands, startling out of her staring.

Ellen looked down to find an in-process bit of dusty red grass weaving, maybe the beginnings of another hat like her guide's.

"Hepp," said the woman, smiling and nodding.

Ellen thought she understood. If she wanted to ask these exceedingly busy people to help her with her problem, it was only fair that she do a little to help them out with their work, too.

Well, now that she'd had a bit of dinner, she didn't feel

quite the urgency to get home straight away. And while she kept her hands busy weaving grass, she could think over how she was going to get home more easily.

What an efficient usage of her time!

Happily, Ellen settled into the weaving, occasionally taking another bite of the remains of her dinner, and thought.

She'd been working for a while when her pocket buzzed.

Startled, she dropped the hat she was weaving. She pawed frantically at her pocket until her fingers touched the folded-up teleporter hat.

When she brought it out and unfolded it, a small green light blinked in irregular patterns on the inside of the hat. The buzzing came in time with the blinks. Ellen stared at it, then suddenly realized that the buzzing was coming from a small speaker, and that, if she strained her ears, she could almost make out someone speaking.

Tentatively, she held the hat closer to her head. She didn't put it on, still wary of being whisked off somewhere even worse than the Moon.

"Hello?" she said. Around her, the alien Moon farmers paused briefly in their various multitasking to blink at her curiously.

"...len? Is tha...ou? ...t's Ris...ko!"

"Risako? Yes, it's me! Risako, your stupid hat took me to the Moon!"

A wave of frustration swept over Ellen. Why hadn't Risako *told* her the teleporter had a built-in communicator? She could have gotten in touch with Little Sister right away, instead of wandering around on the cold, dusty surface of the Moon.

"R...lly? That's so...wesome! Tell m...at it's...ike?"

Ellen shook her head, though she knew Risako couldn't see her. "There's no time for taking data, Little Sister. You've got to help me fix this thing so I can get home in time for school tomorrow."

"Ok...Okay. We'll wor...ogether. I'm getti...eadings from the...leporter. Something's not ri...with the coord...ates."

Ellen rolled her eyes and shared a long-suffering look with the farm boy who had brought her to his family. He was still staring at her with his big black eyes full of obvious wonder as she talked into the teleporter hat.

But the rest of the alien farmers seemed to have gotten over their moment of distraction, and had mostly turned back to their many tasks. The alien mom stepped over to Ellen and the boy, bringing baskets of wadded-up clothes with her.

"Hepp," she said as she plunked the baskets down in front of them.

The boy sighed and reached for his basket.

Ellen nodded, trying to reach for her basket while keeping ahold of her unfinished grass weaving and the teleporter hat.

Risako had continued talking all this time, and Ellen worked on her tasks while she half paid attention to her sister's theorizing through the static.

"Uh-huh, listen, Risako. I've got a lot of stuff on my plate here. Why don't you work on fixing the teleporter by yourself for a bit, and I'll signal you when I've got a free moment in my schedule, okay?"

"Wai...I need your inpu...efore we can account fo...ull to the lef..."

But Ellen could no longer focus on the call, not with both hands full of things to do. And the older alien man was coming around, passing out what looked like bits of wood and tools for carving. Ellen had never carved anything before. Her interest was immediately piqued.

"I'll call you later, Little Sister," she said, and shoved the teleporter hat back into her pocket.

Now, all she had to do was figure out how to manage her weaving, her laundry sorting, and her carving all together.

Juggling all these tasks proved frustrating, especially as she found herself growing more interested in most of them. Even sorting and folding the laundry was made way more interesting than it normally would be by being *alien* laundry. Some of these materials would make some fun, flashy outfits back on Earth, if Ellen could only get the time to work sewing into her busy schedule. Maybe she could shift her piano lesson to a different time? And what if she proposed a change to the exact time of the new anime club?

But even as Ellen considered how this new activity could slot into her already over-filled schedule, she fumbled a few more blades of grass into the hat she was still weaving. She wasn't making much progress, and the sour taste of frustration grew as she took half a second to look over the work she had done so far.

It didn't look very hat-like. She'd barely completed enough weaving for the brim.

And the carving she'd been chipping away at hadn't progressed much beyond "chunk of wood" in the time she'd been turning it over in her hands.

At her feet, the basket of laundry still overflowed with unsorted, unfolded garments.

Unable to help herself, Ellen let out a huff of dissatisfaction. Why couldn't she get any of these things done? She was excited about all of them, just like she was excited about each and every one of her extracurriculars.

She wished she could recreate the amazing focus she'd had during chess club earlier today. Even the teacher who supervised the club had said she'd had amazing focus at this session.

Taking a moment to glance around the farmhouse room, she saw how the rest of the alien family was getting on with all their tasks. Everywhere she looked, aliens were struggling just like she was, tangling themselves up in knitting yarn while trying to play a strange, gray glass Moon flute, or accidentally hammering nails into the shoes they were trying to polish.

Except for the boy. Though he had a number of tasks laid out before him, he was focusing on completing only one task at a time. Only once he'd finished one step of one project did he move to work on another task, except when his mother or father alien gave him a stern look. Then he would work on two jobs together for as long as they were looking. The moment they looked away again, he'd return to one job.

He was making a lot more progress on all of his work than anyone else.

Ellen thought back to her chess club meeting. She'd done so much better today because, with the teleporter *supposedly* taking care of her travel home, she'd been able to focus entirely on the games. Was that the secret? Not hyper-scheduling, not cutting minutes out here and there to make room for yet another activity, but keeping her eye on *one* prize at a time?

But she *liked* all of her activities. How could she choose between chess club and piano lessons, anime club and drama club, swimming lessons and art classes? She wanted to do them all, as well as spend time with her family, watching movies with Mom and Dad and helping Little Sister with her weird science experiments. Especially when those experiments needed Ellen's Responsible Big Sister mode to get the two of them out of trouble, more often than not.

She sighed. She wasn't being a very responsible sister right now. In trying to do everything on her plate, she'd accomplished a whole lot of nothing. She wasn't even trying to help Little Sister figure out how to get the teleporter working to get back home!

Forget choosing between her various clubs. If she stayed here on the Moon, doing three Moon farm tasks at once and failing at all of them, she'd never get to go to *any* of her clubs again!

That thought drove Ellen to her feet. She let the unfinished grass weaving and the wood carving tumble off her lap to clatter on the floor.

Every alien head turned to look at her as she stepped away from their craft circle.

"Sorry," she said, reaching into her pocket for the teleporter hat. "I appreciate you having me over for dinner, but I have to get going now."

The alien mom stood, scowling as she continued to work repairs on a harness for some strange Moon livestock. "Ellln. Hepp."

Ellen shook her head, backing towards the farmhouse door. "I can't help you with your chores anymore. I have to go back to Earth!"

Now the alien dad joined the mom, both wearing "you're grounded" looks on their round, gray faces.

"No rrrf. Ellln hepp. Ellln hepp!"

Ellen had to get away before they tried to send her to her room, any room.

Clutching the teleporter hat in her fist, she turned and ran for the farmhouse door. She yanked it open and jumped outside into the fields of Moon dust. Though the stars looked different on the Moon than they did on Earth, their light reflected off the gray landscape in shimmering waves, lighting Ellen's escape route through the rows of strange crops.

Alien voices called after her, but they got quieter and farther away as she ran on. They weren't chasing her. Maybe they just had too much to do to waste energy following one Earthling girl beyond their farm.

Still, Ellen didn't want to take any chances, so she ran until she was out of breath, focusing only on the movement of her feet through the Moon dust.

She ran well, being so single-minded. The moment she took her attention off the run to look up at the black field of stars through the strange dome that stretched overhead, however, she lost her footing. Tumbling end over end, she rolled down into the small crater she'd dashed straight into. It was everything she could do to hold onto the teleporter hat. Moon dust filled her mouth. As soon as she came to a rest, she spat out as much as she could.

"Ugh, pffthbth," she said. "Blech. I guess that's another mark in favor of keeping my attention on one thing at a time!"

But a quick examination showed she hadn't hurt herself in the fall, and the teleporter wasn't in any worse condition than it had been to start with.

Turning the hat over, she looked for a way to trigger the communication so she could get back in touch with Little Sister.

Try as she might, she couldn't figure it out. The little speaker didn't have any walkie-talkie button that she could find. Frustration mounted again, accompanied this time by a wave of unfairness. She was focusing all her attention on this one thing! Surely, she should be making some sort of progress.

If she couldn't figure this thing out soon, she'd have no choice but to go back to the Moon farm. She'd get hungry again, and thirsty, and it was so cold out here, her teeth were chattering and her fingers were shaking. Now that she wasn't running anywhere, the warmth had drained right out of her body.

She didn't even have the energy to cry.

A crunching sound, like boots in dust, came over the ridge of the crater. Afraid that the farmers had chased her after all, Ellen held her breath.

A moment later, the alien boy popped his head over the ridge and waved down at her. He clambered over the crater edge, slid down the slope of Moon dust as if he were riding a skateboard, and finally came to sit cross-legged across from Ellen. He pulled a strange, pronged Moon tool from his silvery overalls.

"Hepp Ellln," he said, waving the tool at the teleporter hat.

Ellen relaxed, her held breath whooshing out of her. "Thank you so much. If we focus on this together, I'm sure we can get it working again."

The boy nodded. "Foh-kusssss. Rrrf."

Ellen smiled. "You can totally come visit us anytime you need a break from all the activities happening up here. My Little Sister will love you. Now, let's get to work."

The sensation of motion flowed over Ellen, including the pull to the left. But she was expecting it this time, and after the modifications she, the alien farm boy, and Little Sister had made, she knew it wouldn't be anywhere near as inaccurate as the jump that had taken her all the way to the Moon.

She arrived in their backyard, landing behind the garage rather than in the middle of the yard as she'd aimed for. After disentangling herself from the bushes and frightening a poor squirrel, she removed the teleporter hat and trudged up to the back door. Teleporting to the Moon and back was more exhausting than her most extracurricular-packed afternoon.

When she came in through the kitchen door, Mom was there, cleaning up from what looked like a delicious dinner.

"Did you have a good time at the neighbors' house for dinner?" she asked, surprising Ellen. She'd expected to be in trouble.

"Uh, yes. It was... interesting."

Mom turned to look at her, and her eyebrows shot upwards. "You're a mess! Were you doing arts and crafts over there?"

Ellen glanced down at herself. Her clothes were covered in silvery Moon dust, and the teleporter hat was a crumpled ball of construction paper and plastic in her hand.

"Sorry, we got carried away. I'll clean up upstairs."

"Don't forget to do your homework. You've got a busy day tomorrow."

"Actually," Ellen said, brushing Moon dust off onto the mat by the door, "I think I'm going to drop some of my clubs. I've tried out a lot of activities, but it's time to focus on the one or two I really want to pursue."

Mom nodded. "A wise idea. Maybe then you won't be late for dinner again." She smiled, and her eyes twinkled like the stars beyond the dome on the Moon.

Ellen smiled back, gave her clothes one last brush, and dashed upstairs to find Little Sister turning a wrench on the metal prototype in the middle of their bedroom floor.

Little Sister looked up when she came in, but immediately looked away again, clearly steeling herself against being rejected for Ellen's schedule again. "Glad you made it back. I guess you'll be able to get to all your clubs tomorrow after all."

Ellen dropped the teleporter hat and swept Little Sister up into a tight, Responsible Big Sister hug. Little Sister squawked and dropped her wrench, but soon smiled and wrapped her arms around Ellen's neck.

"I'm going to be here to help you with this new prototype, okay?" Ellen said once she put Little Sister back down. "I'm really sorry I blew you off for so long. I guess I forgot that my schedule already had a slot for 'Scientific Adventures with Little Sister' on it, and that's a job that can't be multitasked."

Risako's face lit up in the biggest smile Ellen had seen in a while, and the two of them hugged again.

For the first time all school year, Ellen's calendar had only one thing on it: focus on being the best big sister she could be.

Two

The Incredible Sizemographic Adventure

The hot, sticky air of late summer pulled at Ellen Sugimori's limbs as she dragged herself home from her swimming lessons. All the benefit she'd gotten from the cool, clean water had been ruined within moments of reaching for her towel. She was sweaty, she was tired, and worst of all, she'd been chased by no fewer than three wasps already.

She hated bugs more than anything, and wasps were the absolute worst. Worse even than spiders, because at least spiders couldn't fly.

Her pink *Neko Hime* flip-flops slapped dully against the concrete of the sidewalk as she turned onto her street and trudged the last few blocks to her house.

But when she heard the telltale buzz of insect wings by her ear, a cold zing of instinctive fear shot across her shoulders. Energy crackled through her, and she broke into a run.

Flp-flp-flp! Stupid wasps! Why couldn't they just leave her alone?

Luckily, home and safety lay a few bounding steps ahead. She cleared the front porch, jammed her key into the lock, then yanked the door open all on reflex. Her brain didn't return to ungarbled thoughts until she was inside, leaning against the closed front door, breathing as hard as if she'd run a whole mile. The air-conditioning felt amazing against her overheated skin. The stillness of the air, free of buzzing bugs, sounded like heaven.

"Eriko? Is that you?" came Mom's voice from the living room.

"It's me," Ellen said. She swiped her arm across her sweaty forehead, kicked her flip-flops off in exchange for her house slippers, and moved into the living room. "There was a bug chasing me."

Mom was gathering up her purse when Ellen came in. She was wearing her "running errands" kimono, a traditional Japanese garment that Ellen used to be embarrassed of. But Ellen smiled to see it now.

"You know if you simply remain calm, the bugs won't bother you," Mom said.

"I know, I know," Ellen said. But she simply couldn't remain calm whenever that ominous buzzing filled the air. She couldn't help the immediate response. What if the next wasp stung her?

Mom stepped close, wrapped an arm around Ellen's shoulders, and dropped a kiss on her forehead. "I'm running out to the hardware store to pick up some things for the renovations. I'll be back in an hour. Please try not to fight with your sister again?"

Ellen bit back a sigh. "I'll try." With the way things had been going lately, trying was all she could promise. Despite

Ellen's best efforts to be a good, responsible big sister, she and Little Sister ended up fighting almost every day now.

Mom kissed her again, then swept elegantly to the door. Ellen winced as the door swung open, just in case the wasp was waiting for her out there. But nothing buzzed in, not even a simple fly.

Once Mom was gone, Ellen headed upstairs. She wanted a nice, cool shower to wash all the chlorine out of her hair and the sweat from her skin. Plus, she wouldn't be able to fight with Risako if she was too busy showering.

Upstairs, the door of the bedroom she and Little Sister shared stood open as it had all week. The stack of cardboard boxes full of Mom and Dad's stuff from their bedroom had grown, and now even a couple of boxes had spilled out into the hallway. Mom and Dad needed the space temporarily while they made renovations to their bedroom. Ellen didn't mind too much, but it did make getting in and out of her space rather a tight squeeze. It also made it harder to avoid bumping into— often literally—Little Sister.

Ellen sucked in her tummy to get past the boxes in the doorway. She'd get in, excavate a path to her dresser for fresh clothes, and squeeze back out again for the shower.

The window on the far side of the bedroom was open, letting a thin, hot breeze set the pink and white *Neko Hime* curtains swaying and rasping as they caught on cardboard edges.

Little Sister was here, standing among the stacked boxes by her science table. Ellen could tell she was Doing Science even though she wasn't wearing her usual white lab coat, goggles, or gloves. They'd all been buried in the closet, which was blocked in by yet another stack of boxes. But Risako's stance was unmistakable, as was the way Ellen's tummy twisted in apprehension at the sight of those determined shoulders and hunched back.

No first-grader should be able to look that determined, Ellen thought. It wasn't natural.

But then, Little Sister's science wasn't exactly what she could call natural, either. Little Sister's cardboard contraptions worked in mysterious ways and had gotten the two of them into more scrapes and close calls than Ellen wanted to count. Luckily, Mom and Dad had never found out about these adventures. Luckily for Little Sister, anyway.

With the high tensions between Ellen and Little Sister right now, Ellen knew an experiment would be more than enough to spark another fight. She determined not to acknowledge the presence of science in her bedroom this time. She just wanted to take a shower.

Risako looked up and nodded at Ellen. "Hey."

Ellen nodded back. "Hello." There, that was perfectly polite. She put her swim bag on her bed, then waded through the boxes to her dresser. Risako seemed content to leave their greetings at that, as she'd turned back to whatever she was working on. Ellen didn't want to know what it was, so she worked to keep her eyes on her drawer of cute shirts.

Still, a flash of sunlight bouncing off something reflective drew her gaze.

A clear plastic thin rectangular container stood on Risako's science table next to whatever cardboard contraption Risako was working on. It was full of something like dirt or sand, and a bunch of branching tunnels like plant roots wound through the dirt. Inside those tunnels, little black specks were moving—

"Risako!" Ellen shouted. "Is that—did you—*why are there bugs in my room?*"

The panicky, tight feeling was back in her shoulders, and she realized she'd backed herself up against the dresser as if pressing herself against its solid wood might keep any creepy crawlies from touching her.

Annoyingly, Little Sister looked calm, even a little excited.

"Aren't they neat? Mom and Dad got me this ant farm. I'm going to study how their hive mind works and apply it to—"

"No," Ellen said. "You're going to take those things outside right now and dump them in the garden."

Little Sister frowned. "That's not fair. It's my room, too. Why can't I have some pets? Mom and Dad said I could."

"Yeah, well, Mom and Dad don't know you only wanted them to experiment on them. And I don't care if it's your room, too. I am *not* sleeping in a room where ants might crawl all over me!"

"I'm not going to hurt them, and they're not going to crawl on you," Little Sister said. "I just need to collect some data with my Sizemograph." She stepped aside and gestured at the thing she'd been working on. It looked like a repurposed water rifle combined with a shoebox and an exorbitant amount of thick, silvery tape.

Ellen shook her head. She didn't want to know what a Sizemograph was, though she suspected it had nothing to do with earthquakes. She just wanted to take a shower, put on some fresh clothes, and relax in a room with no bugs in it.

She also wanted to keep from fighting with Little Sister. She was tired of it, and she'd promised Mom she would try not to.

And the only way she could think of to avoid a fight right this minute was to do something drastic. Something she'd never, ever done before.

Mom hadn't left for the hardware store yet. Ellen hadn't heard the car start.

She took a deep breath. "Risako, I need you to get rid of those bugs, or I am going to go downstairs and *tell* on you."

Risako's eyes went round as teacups. Her mouth hung open in a silent gasp of affront. Neither sister moved.

Then Risako closed her mouth with a firm snap, and her eyes turned hard.

"Mom and Dad gave me these ants. I am not throwing them away."

Ellen stuck out her chin. "Fine. I'm telling."

She turned to begin the process of squeezing through the boxes.

Little Sister grabbed the Sizemograph from her science table and brought it up to her shoulder. She pumped the water rifle's action a few times, sending its hollow, plasticky *whup-whup-whup* echoing among the stacks of boxes.

Ellen sucked in her tummy and tried to sidestep between the boxes faster.

Little Sister squeezed the trigger. A sharp click came from across the room, then a warm, tingling sensation struck Ellen's shoulders.

The next thing she knew, the boxes around her were getting bigger, taller, farther apart. She stumbled on strands of carpet that were tangling over her feet.

In another blink of an eye, Ellen stood as tall as... as an ant!

Little Sister's footsteps shook the floor like miniature earthquakes, and Ellen clung to a strand of carpet for dear life. A moment later, a low whooshing sound filled the air, and Risako's enormous face swooped down to peer at Ellen from above.

"Hold still," said Way Too Big Sister.

Ellen, trembling with fear at her suddenly diminished size, couldn't have moved if she'd wanted to. Thus, she was a prime target for the giant pair of tweezers the Entirely Too Large Risako picked her up with.

To Risako's credit, the metal prongs closed gently on the back of Ellen's swim shirt without pinching even a little bit.

Wind rushed past Ellen's ears as she found herself lifted up and up and up, until she was dangling right before Risako's mountain-sized nose. Risako looked at her cross-eyed.

That ridiculous image was enough to shock Ellen out of her momentary paralysis.

"You put me down right now and make me normal-sized again!" she screamed, shaking a finger at Little Sister. Her voice came out tinny, but she could tell Little Sister heard her from the way those gargantuan eyes narrowed.

"First, you have to promise not to tell on me."

"No! I am *so* telling on you now. You didn't even ask if you could shrink me before doing it! You *never* ask, Risako. It's way past time I told."

Anger ran hot through Ellen's tiny body. She made tiny fists and heaved air in and out of her tiny lungs.

But Risako seemed unmoved by Ellen's fury. Instead of looking sorry for her actions, she shook her head. "If I asked, you would always say no. But I need your help with my experiments, Ellen. Besides, it's not like I don't take part in them, too. Here."

She took booming giant steps back to her science table. Ellen, still dangling from the tweezers, twisted in the breeze of motion. She also got a good glimpse out the window, where Mom's car was pulling out of the driveway.

"Mom!" she yelled. "Mooooom!"

But her tinny voice was too weak to reach across the distance, and Mom drove away.

Little Sister swung the tweezers over the science table and began to lower them. To Ellen's horror, she realized her feet were swinging above the plastic lid of the ant farm.

"Don't you dare—"

"There, just sit there for a moment while I get my equipment together and shrink myself."

"What? No, don't do that!"

But Risako ignored her. She collected a full-to-bursting backpack from the floor and looped her arms through the straps. Whatever was inside it clattered in a muffled sort of way, making Ellen even more nervous. What could Little Sister possibly have in there? What kind of tiny science was she up to?

Ellen had to put a stop to this craziness. "Risako, I mean it, don't shrink yourself, or we'll be in big trouble!"

Little Sister gave no indication that she'd heard Ellen as she climbed on top of the science table, her scrambling motions setting the table and everything on it rattling. The ant farm wobbled like a ship tossed on the ocean. Ellen clung to the lid, her eyes closed tightly.

Risako sat cross-legged next to the ant farm. "Here, Ellen, come hold this in place."

Ellen cracked one eye open. Risako had propped a long piece of wood against the side of the once-again-steady ant farm. A closer look showed it to be a tiny ladder made of toothpicks.

Ellen had just enough time to consider scrambling down that ladder and away from the churning swarm of ants below her before Risako picked up her Sizemograph and pointed it directly at herself.

Ellen gasped in horror. "Risako, no! We'll be trapped—"

Too late. The *click* ricocheted off the stacks of boxes, and the warm, slightly orange ray of the Sizemograph radiated towards Risako's chest.

Ellen watched unblinking as Risako shrank and the Sizemograph tumbled to land on their bedroom floor, practically miles below either of them.

"Oh, Little Sister," she moaned. "You've done it this time."

Little Sister, now of a proper size relative to Ellen once

again, seemed unaware of the danger they were in as she clambered up the rickety toothpick ladder and joined Ellen at the top of the ant farm.

"What?" she said, panting.

Ellen ground her teeth to keep from shouting. "How do you intend for us to regain our proper sizes when the...the *Sizemograph* is all the way down there?"

Little Sister blinked, peered over the edge, and blinked some more.

"Why didn't you tell me not to shrink myself?" she finally blurted.

Ellen gaped. "I *did*. I said we'd be in big trouble!"

"I thought you meant with Mom and Dad! I didn't think you meant about making sure the Sizemograph would stay in reach!"

Now Ellen did shout, a wordless scream of frustration. "That's the problem with you. You never think far enough ahead before barreling forward with your experiments, and it always gets us in trouble! I'm tired of it, Risako. I hope you realize now that it doesn't matter if I tell Mom and Dad anymore. One of them is going to have to help us, which means they'll figure everything out for themselves."

The idea sent a strange shot of loss through Ellen, but she ignored it. She would be happy if her life never involved Little Sister's science again.

Risako pouted for a moment. Then she shook herself and smiled.

"I'm sure we can find a way back to our original sizes before Mom and Dad get home. And the only way back is through! Down we go, then. Onward to research!"

She hitched her backpack on her shoulders, then tromped off towards the end of the ant farm, where a section of the plastic lid would lift on a hinge to allow access.

Ellen crossed her arms over her chest. "Oh, no. No way. I am not going down there." No way, no how, no chance. No bugs, especially not bugs that were now, relatively, giant.

Little Sister shrugged and didn't look back at Ellen. "Suit yourself. You can sit up here all by yourself and watch for spiders."

She flicked the latch, and the lid lifted with an ominous, plasticky creak.

Ellen spluttered for breath, her back straight as a steel rod. "Sp-sp-*spiders?*"

"There's a mama spider up in the corner of the ceiling who'd probably like some ants for when her babies hatch." Little Sister gestured over her head vaguely.

The idea of baby spiders—a million, billion baby spiders in one egg sac, probably!—sent such a chill through Ellen that she found herself crossing the ant farm lid without even thinking about it.

"I am not waiting by myself for spiders to come get me," she said, rubbing her arms to get warm again.

"Then I guess you'll have to come help me with my research. Come on, Ellen, these are just ants. They won't hurt you. They don't even have stingers."

Ellen peered down into the ant farm. She didn't see any ants on the surface, at least. The dirt inside lay a bit of a drop down, but Little Sister was uncoiling a rope from her backpack.

Little Sister affixed the rope to the hinge of the lid. Then she tossed the other end down into the farm. It fluttered there, brushing the topmost grains of dirt.

"Time to climb down," said Little Sister in a too-cheerful voice.

Ellen cast one longing glance over her shoulder at the open bedroom door. It was so far away, and neither Mom nor Dad stood in it with a ready rescue. Then her eyes slid up to the corner of the ceiling. Was it this shadowy corner where the mama spider spun her web? Ellen shivered again.

"All right," she said. "I guess we're going down after all."

Ellen's house slippers crunched softly into the ant farm dirt. The grains were as big as gravel pebbles to her now, and standing on them in such inadequate footwear was already making her feet hurt.

It was warm inside, and a little humid, thanks to the sun's rays filtering through the plastic.

Little Sister surveyed the thin strip of landscape with one hand over her eyes. "There's the entrance to the tunnels," she said, pointing.

Ellen looked. Sure enough, a dark, gaping maw opened in the dirt a few strides off. She thought she heard something uttering a low moan from its depths.

"Ugh," she said.

"Let's go," Little Sister said. Once again, she hitched her backpack up on her shoulders, then set off like an explorer striding across the savannah on safari. In fact, Ellen wondered why she didn't have a pith helmet on.

Not wanting to be left behind, Ellen fought against the instincts screaming at her to stay away from the dark tunnel and scrambled to catch up. She caught hold of Little Sister's arm just as Little sister was flicking on a flashlight from her backpack.

The light cut a swath through the darkness as she swept it across the entrance, reflecting off glittering bits of dirt and casting shadows against the grainy walls. A smell wafted out of the darkness, not exactly unpleasant, but kind of like a mix of old vegetables and something sticky-sweet like maple syrup left open too long.

Ellen let out a laugh that was far too breathy. "Heh, I guess there aren't any ants lying in wait to ambush us—*aah!*"

The flashlight's beam fell on a gleaming black form, revealing long, spindly legs, twitchy antennae, and an alien face of sharp angles and clicking mandibles. A pair of enormous, many-faceted eyes stared dully at the two sisters as the ant marched out of the tunnel entrance towards them.

The ant waved its antennae over Little Sister's body. Little Sister stood as still as a statue.

Ellen, panicking, stumbled backwards, fully intending to flee. But her heel caught on a large grain of dirt, and she sat down hard. Dirt scored her palms, but she barely felt the sting of it in her fear.

The ant opened its sharp mandibles with a sound like a pair of scissors opening.

"Risako!"

The ant was going to eat her sister! There was no way Ellen was going to let that happen. She fumbled behind her, groping for a clod of dirt big enough to clobber the ant with.

"Hold on, Risako," she said. Her fingers closed on a big piece, and she levered herself up onto one knee.

But Risako was laughing and reaching to pet the ant!

"Hello, friend! I've come to study you. Here, let's just put this on you, okay?"

Amazed, Ellen watched as Little Sister rummaged in her backpack, then pulled out a cardboard helmet of some kind from among what appeared to be a collection of them. Two squares had been scribbled on the front in crayon, one red and one green, like signal lights.

"Risako, what on Earth is that?"

"It's a hive-mind wave reader," Risako explained as she clipped the helmet onto the ant's head. It nestled between the antennae and made the ant look like it was ready to go ride bikes with its friends.

Ellen shuddered at the image of too many legs pedaling down her street.

"Anyway," Risako was saying. "We need to get these helmets onto as many of the colony as we can. That's how I'll get the best data and discover how the ants make the most efficient use of their tunnel space. I figure we could apply it to our room while Mom and Dad have all their stuff in our way. Maybe then you and I could quit fighting all the time."

She turned to face Ellen by the end of her explanation, and her face showed something Ellen didn't often see there: uncertainty.

Ellen sighed. "That's very thoughtful of you. But I still wish you'd asked me before shrinking me. You know how much bugs give me the creeps. This is really uncomfortable for me."

She couldn't help glancing back at the ant. Its shiny black exoskeleton and blank-looking eyes made her skin tingle with revulsion.

But... it did seem docile enough. In fact, the way it was running its antennae over Risako kind of reminded Ellen of when the neighborhood cats would rub up against her legs. Little Sister giggled and scratched the side of the ant's head.

Ellen shook her head. No, she did not find ants cute, not even a little bit!

"Here, Ellen. He wants to say hi to you!"

Ellen chewed on her lip, torn with indecision. But the ant waved its antennae at her, and a gleam of sunlight hit its eyes just right to make them look happy and playful.

With her heart pounding in her throat, Ellen edged closer to the enormous ant. Her fingers shook as she reached for it.

"See? It's okay, Ellen," said Little Sister.

Ellen let out a surprised laugh. The ant's body was hard to the touch, like a mix between plastic and glass. The antennae tickled as they danced over her arms and face.

"Let's go into the tunnels and find more of them," said Little Sister, and Ellen found herself nodding.

They walked through the tunnels, guided both by Little Sister's flashlight and by the knowing lead of their ant guide. Whenever the tunnel branched, he chose a path without hesitation. Gradually, the three of them descended into the depths of the ant farm.

Along the way, they ran into other ants. Each time, the first ant would greet the newcomers with waving antennae and clicking mandibles, then the new ant would wave its antennae over Risako and Ellen. Ellen would pet the ant in growing wonder while Little Sister put one of her hive-mind wave reader helmets on it. Finally, the ant would trundle away, off to do whatever chores it must be working on for the good of the colony.

Or off to ride bikes with the rest of the helmeted crew. Ellen giggled at the thought.

"What?" asked Little Sister as they went deeper into the tunnels.

"Just a funny thought. I never imagined ants would be so friendly. I've always thought of them as, well, gross. Sorry," Ellen added, wincing at their ant guide.

The ant twitched an antenna as if to say "I get that all the time."

Little Sister got her backpack, now significantly emptier, up on one shoulder. "Ants are important members of our environment. They do all sorts of work to help keep trash and stuff we humans don't want around under control. And they do it all using their amazing hive-mind to cooperate!"

Ellen couldn't help it. She smiled along with Risako, feeling her enthusiasm infect her. Who'd have ever thought she'd come to smile about any kind of bug?

Beside them, the first ant came to a halt so suddenly his feet sent bits of dirt rolling ahead. His antennae went still, and his mandibles gave one sharp click.

The helmet on his head flashed, the crayon squares lighting up in rapid sequence.

Little Sister went stiff as cardboard herself. "Uh-oh."

Ellen didn't like that, not one bit. The tight, panicky feeling came back into her shoulders.

And not a moment too soon, because the ant broke free of its standstill, only to clamp its mandibles around Ellen's middle and haul her off down the dark tunnel!

"Aaaah! Let go, let go! Risakooooo!"

Ellen writhed in the ant's mandibles, her swim shirt catching on the serrated edges. She managed to turn enough to look back up the tunnel. But all she saw before darkness swallowed her was Risako standing in the light of her flashlight, one hand stretched after Ellen and the ant.

Behind Risako, a pair of helmeted ants closed in, flashing tiny blips of red and green.

Ellen had no idea how long the ant carried her through the dark tunnels. Without vision, she lost all sense of time. But the ant was hurrying, as evident by the thunderous patter of its six feet.

The panic hadn't left Ellen, that was for sure. Her whole body was taut as a wire. But so far the ant held her gently. His mandibles snagged on her swim shirt, but he hadn't cut her at all.

Finally, after mere minutes or hours, the ant dropped into a lower tunnel with a surprisingly lithe leap. Ellen bit back a yelp.

She blinked hard a few times, then realized she could see vague outlines of the tunnel walls.

Up ahead, something was giving off a bit of light.

The smell of the tunnels grew stronger here, and Ellen wrinkled her nose at it. Leaves left in puddles long after a rainstorm is what it smelled like, mixed with honey, maybe. She wouldn't want to spread it on her toast, anyway.

The ant carried her onward into the dim light. The tunnel opened into a cavern swarming with ants, some helmeted, most not. As the ants moved, they alternately blocked and unblocked the source of the dim light: lots of round, whitish ovals speckled in the walls, carefully tended by special worker ants.

Ant eggs! From the brief glances Ellen got, there must be hundreds of them down here waiting to hatch, and a frenzied swarm of grown-up ants to meet them when they did.

Ellen's ant trundled straight into the center of the swarm.

"Ugh! Stop it, don't touch me," Ellen cried. The ants waved their antennae over her in a mass of twirling, tickling touches. Ellen's skin crawled at the sensation. Tears pricked behind her eyes. What were these horrible, gross, terrifying bugs going to do to her down here?

As if the thought was a cue, her ant opened its mandibles with a loud snick, and Ellen tumbled to the ground. Ellen scrambled to curl herself into a tiny ball, arms over her head, knees tucked into her tummy.

"Please don't eat me, please don't eat me," she chanted, swallowing against the sobs trying to escape her throat.

The ants seemed to listen to her. With a rustle of exoskeletons, the ants moved away from her. Ellen lifted one arm a tiny bit to peek out into the dim cave.

Thud. Thud. Thud.

The dirt pebbles rattled next to Ellen's cheek, and out of the dimness came the biggest ant Ellen had ever seen. Her triangular face was glossier than the others, and her huge abdomen was a pale yellowish color. The smell of her as she approached, spicy and musty, clogged Ellen's throat.

Ellen didn't need to take in the way the other ants bowed to this one to know she was in the presence of the Queen.

And the Queen was reaching with both her antennae to brush Ellen's arms and face.

"Uh, Y-y-your M-m-m-majesty," Ellen said, uncurling enough to sit up. Maybe the Queen meant to eat her, but Ellen didn't think so. Still, the tightness remained in her shoulders, and she sat with them hunched around her ears.

The Queen motioned with one leg, and a pair of ants stepped forward. They carried one of Little Sister's helmets between them. Another motion from the Queen, and the two carefully placed the helmet on Ellen's head.

The moment it was settled in place, a multitude of voices whispered inside her mind.

/march for get food/

/march for store food/

/march for feed Queen/

These whispers buzzed constantly, a repeating drone that would become hypnotic if Ellen let it. But there were other voices, other commands moving through the hive-mind.

/danger, intrusion/

/march for fight enemy!/

Fear flooded through Ellen at that, and she clamped down on whatever it was that allowed the whispers into her head.

The ants thought she and Little Sister were enemies! They'd separated her from her sister in order to divide and conquer! And if Ellen ever wanted to see her proper size again, let alone live to fight with Little Sister another day, she'd have to get over her fear of bugs and fight her way through this swarm and their Queen.

"Oh, Risako," she moaned. But she got to her feet and made a pair of fists. It wasn't much of a weapon at all, but it was all she had to defend herself with.

The Queen waved her antennae in a distinct shushing motion. Ellen was so shocked to see such a human gesture from that monstrous thing that she opened her mind back up to the chatter in the helmet.

/Calm yourself, tiny thing, but do not lose your fear. Feel the vibrations coming from above!/

The Queen's voice was mellow and full of what Ellen's choir teacher called "round tones." It made her sound sophisticated, and Ellen found herself almost wanting to obey her. Carefully, Ellen tipped her head to "feel the vibrations."

At first, all she heard was the clicking of mandibles, the rasp of exoskeletons, and the thumping of her own heart. She listened harder.

High above, through the layers of dirt, something other than Ellen and Risako had intruded into the ant farm. The acoustics of the tunnels carried the whirring of insect wings all the way down into the depths of this cavern.

"A wasp!" Ellen gasped. At once, she remembered the open window, the fluttering curtains, and the wasp that had chased her home from the pool. She and Little Sister had left the lid of the ant farm open, and now that wasp had come inside, looking for an ant-sized snack.

/I sensed that you were not well-equipped to defend yourself, tiny thing, and thus directed my workers to bring you down here where you could be kept safe during the battle./

A wave of gratitude swept over Ellen. Even through all these layers of dirt, that distinctive wasp buzz had her scared. She realized the ants weren't scary at all, and never had been, even when they were bigger than her.

But the wasp posed a real threat, especially with Ellen and Little Sister being shrunken down, and—

"Oh no, Little Sister is still up there!"

The panic she'd felt earlier rushed back, but this time it carried the sharp tang of determination. Just as she'd been willing to stand up to the Queen ant for a slim chance at reuniting with Risako, Ellen knew she'd face a ginormous wasp with her bare fists if she had to.

Still, she wished she *didn't* have to. Cold fear had her working her jaw to keep her teeth from chattering.

The Queen's soothing voice came to her again. /Your sibling is far more useful to us at the front lines with my workers. Feel for yourself, tiny thing./

Ellen listened hard, not with her ears this time, but through the helmet and the whispered chatter it allowed her to hear. Beyond the simple whispers of commands to follow was Risako's voice, cutting through the din like an explorer's machete through the jungle.

/Risako!/ Ellen mind-shouted.

/Ellen! Don't come up topside, there's a big ol' wasp buzzing around up here./

/I know. Are you fighting it? Be careful!/ Ellen's throat closed despite the confident sound of Little Sister's mental voice. Neither of them had fought a giant wasp before. Little Sister could be stung!

Ellen realized her hands were clenching and unclenching. She couldn't just sit down here in the dark, safe and sound with the Queen and her eggs, while Little Sister put herself in danger.

There had to be something she could do to help fight off the wasp.

/My workers are brave, and there are multitudes of them,/ said the Queen. /But they lack much ability to think for themselves. Even I am not so good at solving such involved problems as this one when compared to you and your sibling. Perhaps you could lend us your mind in this fight?/

Yes! The suggestion brought a cool splash of relief to Ellen's frantic nerves, just like jumping into the pool on a hot summer day.

Except...

"My sister and I have been fighting a lot lately. I don't know if she'll want to take directions from me."

/Disputes do happen, even amongst the closest knit colonies. We who are used to living in tight quarters have perfected the art of apology and understanding. Our shared mind helps, of course./

Ellen nodded in understanding. These ants, living in such narrow tunnels and darkness, had to have a good handle on working through their little arguments. One couldn't have two ants snipping at each other as they passed each other in the tiny corridors, or everything would get jammed up. A single ant might be tiny, but even two or three together could create a huge problem.

A sudden idea flashed in Ellen's mind, and as she clapped her hands in surprise, the thought rippled through her helmet and across the entire colony.

/That's it! An individual ant might be too tiny to threaten a wasp, but everyone can band together to make a humongous.../

Ellen sent a mental picture of her idea and got a murmur of understanding from the ants in return.

Little Sister's voice came loud and clear, too. /But I had an idea to repurpose some of these helmets into a prototype weapon of some kind so each ant can fight on their own—/

But Ellen shook her head. /We'll fight this invasion better if we work together, Little Sister. We have to remember that we're on the same team, that the real problem is coming from outside the two of us./

Ellen felt Risako's wispy thoughts of understanding. They were both picturing their bedroom and the way their nicely divided spaces had been squished together with Mom and Dad's stuff clogging up the place. Clashes were inevitable in such a situation.

Little Sister sighed. /You're right, and—and I'm sorry for fighting with you about stupid stuff./

/It's okay, and I'm sorry, too,/ said Ellen. /But we can work it out better once this wasp is dealt with./

/Right! Roger! I'll send you status reports on the lay of the dirt. You tell the troops how to advance,/ said Little Sister.

Steeling her nerves, Ellen prepared to command the ant army against her biggest fear.

The battlefield didn't exactly smolder, but the hot air inside the ant farm shimmered with the vibrations from the intruding wasp's wings. The strange vegetable smell of the ants mingled with a metallic tang that clung to the wasp. The buzz of flight, the swish of the stinger, the snick-snick of a hundred mandibles wove together to create a deafening thunder.

Little Sister held a defensive line against the wasp, keeping her ants firmly stacked into a barrier the stabbing stinger couldn't get through. Meanwhile, another cluster of ants clambered on top of one another into something a little more sophisticated.

Ellen got all this through her connection to the hive-mind. She remained safe and cool in the dim egg cavern, her back resting against the Queen's abdomen as she focused all her energy on directing the formation of the ants' main weapon.

/Swat Team, form up!/ she called.

She sent another image of a thick, flat swatting surface.

Another platoon of ants swarmed up the already half-constructed swatter, scrambling into their places.

Ellen double checked their placement. She nudged a couple of ants into more stable spots.

/Okay, Risako! It's your turn now./

Risako commanded her ants with the ease of a career general. /Operation Separate! Make room!/

Like a fleet of battle bots, the ants in the defensive line split into two groups. Both groups then broke into smaller bunches, and these bunches rushed for the safety of the tunnels. But they weren't retreating.

/Operation Block the Way!/ cried Little Sister.

The ants dispersed throughout the tunnels, forming clumps of three and four ants each at strategic locations among the branching paths. Each blockage represented another barrier the wasp would have to get through in order to reach the Queen and her eggs, should it manage to evade the Swat Team.

But Ellen intended to swat that wasp good and hard. It deserved it after the way it had chased her home and tried to terrorize these innocent ants.

/All blocked,/ said Little Sister.

/Okay, Swat Team,/ Ellen commanded. /On my signal, begin swatting!/

The giant wasp-swatter made of ants surged forward.

The wasp buzzed its ugly brown wings and bared its mandibles. Ellen glared at it through the eyes of her ant platoon. She had to time her swat carefully, or she'd simply give the wasp an opening to dart around her.

The ants' anticipation quivered through her mind in time with the harsh beats of the wasp's wings, urging Ellen to give the command now, now, now! She felt that familiar tightness creeping into her shoulders where they rested against the Queen.

But she also felt the Queen's steady presence and Little Sister's constant support.

Drawing a deep breath through her nose, Ellen kept her entire focus locked on the wasp. She would not let it scare her this time!

She watched, waiting for the perfect moment...

The wasp landed on the plastic side of the ant farm, tired out from all its buzzing. Its yellow-and-black head pointed down towards the dirt. Its mandibles hung open in a hiss of anger.

/NOW!/ Ellen shouted.

The ants moved as one, and the swatter swung. Time seemed to slow to a crawl as it swept through its arc.

Closer...

The wasp twitched its wings, about to take flight. Ellen tensed.

Closer...

Risako gave an order to her ants, calling for a distraction. Ants poured from the tunnels, forming themselves into mockeries of wasps, pulling their mandibles wide in silly grins and twirling their antennae like they couldn't figure out up from down.

/Nyaaaah!/ called the ants over the hive-mind.

The wasp paused. It turned its head.

Splat!

Pure, vindictive joy flowed through the entire colony, starting with Ellen's front-line ants and rushing all the way to the dark cavern where she and the Queen lay. Ellen basked in it, and in her own triumph, as her Swat Team peeled themselves away from the battle zone.

Thick, gooey bug juice dripped down the clear plastic of the ant farm.

/You have earned a commendation of the highest order, you

and your sibling,/ said the Queen in her soothing tones. /Anything you wish, if it is in the power of my colony to give it to you, will be yours./

Ellen smiled, and as Little Sister's excited whoop came over the hive-mind helmet, her smile grew wider. She knew Little Sister was of the same mind as she was.

/Thank you, Your Majesty. I think there's only one thing my sister and I need right now. If your ants will follow my orders one more time, we can construct a big grabber to get my sister's Sizemograph up off the floor and return us to our original sizes./

The Queen bowed her triangular head in solemn approval.

Ellen's first instinct upon regaining her proper size was to rush to the open window and slam it closed. But her impulse was checked first by the stacks and stacks of boxes of Mom and Dad's stuff blocking her way, and second by the realization that she didn't want to let her fear of wasps and other bugs keep her from enjoying a nice summer breeze.

Behind her, Little Sister grunted as her own re-growth brought her banging against the boxes beside her science table. "Ugh, these stupid boxes! I'm so tired of them."

"Me, too," said Ellen. "And they're definitely not helping us share our space well. We never used to fight so much before Mom and Dad invaded our room."

"Yeah. Ellen, I really am sorry about the ants. If you're uncomfortable, we can get rid of them. I'll just do any more experiments with the Sizemograph outside."

Ellen smiled, then shook her head. "Nah, the ants can stay. They're not so bad, and besides, it *is* your room, too. And I'm sorry for threatening to tell on you. Mom and Dad don't need to know about *all* of your experiments."

She glanced out the window. The sun was a little closer to the horizon than it had been before their tiny adventure began, but not much closer. Mom wouldn't be back from the hardware store yet. Dad would be at work for another while, too.

Ellen grinned at Little Sister.

"I think Mom and Dad have had their stuff in our room long enough. What do you say we work together like our ant friends and drive the invaders out of our colony?"

Little Sister answered with a grin of her own, one which she usually reserved for Doing Science. "Commence Operation Expand the Tunnels!"

Together, they heaved and pushed and panted and sweated, shifting boxes until they could see their whole carpet again, open their closet door all the way, and reach their dressers without twisting themselves unnaturally. By the time they finished, Ellen needed that long-abandoned shower more than ever. Her hair stuck to her forehead in sweaty clumps, and her swim shirt clung to her back like a second skin. Little Sister was breathing hard, her cheeks flushed.

But Ellen was too busy surveying their work, feeling proud and victorious, to go get a shower now. Besides, she didn't need to avoid Little Sister so much now.

A tell-tale buzzing came whirring by her ear.

Risako gasped. "The window! Hold still, Ellen, I'll—"

Whap!

Ellen hopped on one foot to get her house slipper back on. "Got 'im. Gotta protect our ants, right?"

Little Sister smirked. "Gotta protect our room."

And when Mom and Dad got home, they'd find the Sugimori Sisters standing as a united front against any attempts to re-invade.

THREE

The Unmitigated Birthday Disaster

With a gusty sigh of contentment, Ellen Sugimori twirled in front of the mirror in the bedroom she shared with Little Sister. The dress she wore was special, made of a soft fabric dyed Ellen's favorite shade of green, carefully sewed into existence over the past few weeks by Mom. Her skirt flared around her legs, making the pretty sparkles of sequins glint in the light from the ceiling fan.

She smiled wide as she completed the turn and the skirt settled again. It truly did make her feel like a princess, just as she'd imagined. All it lacked was a silver tiara, and maybe a pair of black shoes shined until she could see her face in them. The shoes she had down in the closet by the front door. The tiara she'd have to do without. Maybe some of her sparkly hair clips would do the trick?

She gathered her black hair into a pile on top of her head,

turning this way and that, and squinted at her reflection. Whatever she chose to do with her hair would have to be *perfect*.

Today was Ellen Sugimori's eleventh birthday.

She hadn't asked for a whole-day celebration the way she used to when she was a little kid, but a girl didn't turn eleven every birthday. She still wanted things to be special. Perfect.

Grown up.

Mom would be making a special birthday dinner for her tonight, and even Little Sister wouldn't be allowed to complain about it. Not that Ellen felt smug about this small victory. She was much too responsible to gloat. Mom, Dad, and Little Sister would dress up all fancy, and the whole family would have a glamorous, elegant dinner worthy of Ellen's new level of maturity.

Secretly, Ellen was excited to be the prettiest of the whole family. It *was* her birthday, after all.

To that end, she twisted her hair into a different style, holding it in place while she examined it from every angle to see if it looked princess-y enough.

A soft knock came at the open bedroom door. "Ellen? Are you busy?"

Ellen turned to see Little Sister standing in the doorway. Little Sister wore a bright, excited expression.

She also wore her white science lab coat and the pair of thick black rubber gloves that made up her Mad Scientist uniform. One arm was tucked behind her back, clearly hiding something.

Ellen pursed her lips and let her hair tumble back around her shoulders. "I'm trying out hairstyles for tonight. I definitely don't have time to help you with any experiments today, Risako, which I think I remember reminding you of yesterday?"

Ellen didn't want to be selfish or anything, but the last thing she wanted happening on her birthday was one of Little Sister's strange, uncontrollable experiments ruining things. No matter whether it was the cardboard rocket ship blasting them out of Earth orbit or the still-on-the-fritz pipe-cleaner time machine shoving them through the gloop of time to face down dinosaurs in the past or strangers from the future, Ellen could count on them having one effect for sure: they'd all absolutely destroy her beautiful new dress.

Little Sister scuffed the toe of one of her house slippers against the carpet. The excited glow hadn't left her cheeks despite Ellen's set-down. "I have a present for you, though. It's in the kitchen."

Ellen's sense of self-preservation—honed to sharpness with all the misadventures Risako's experiments had dragged her through—remained alert. "A present? In the kitchen?"

"Yes!" Apparently losing her ability to keep the secret, Little Sister waved her one hand as she spoke. The other remained behind her back, but her shoulder trembled as if barely managing to hold back a landslide. "I'm going to create a chemical solution which will make your birthday dinner taste even better. Well? Are you surprised?"

Ellen tried to smile but was pretty sure she only stretched her lips into a thin line. She wasn't thrilled to receive this "present," and to be honest she wasn't all that surprised, either. Little Sister could be counted on to turn to science for everything, even when she'd been explicitly asked not to.

Still, the grown-up thing to do would be to thank Little Sister for her thoughtfulness.

"Risako, um..."

"I know you asked for no experiments, but you don't have to worry!" Little Sister said. She spoke in a rush, her words cramming together in her haste to explain herself. "I'm not using one of my own prototypes for this. It's a chemistry set Mom and Dad gave me for Christmas, see? Really, it's barely even science. I'm just following the directions, step by step."

She brought her hidden hand out from behind her back to reveal the box the chemistry set had come in. Its colorful design of a boy and girl wearing thick plastic goggles and making wide-eyed gasps over a set of test tubes did jog Ellen's memory.

"Oh," she said, blinking. "I... well. It's very thoughtful of you to use your own present for me."

Little Sister's grin widened, and she bounced on the balls of her feet as if today were *her* birthday. "I thought this would both play to my strengths and be something nice and predictable for you on your birthday. So? Will you come downstairs so I can do the 'experiment' and get you your taste-enhancing solution before Mom gets home and needs the kitchen?"

Seeing Little Sister's clear desire to make Ellen happy with this present, well, *did* make Ellen happy. With an elegant swish of her skirt, Ellen stepped forward to clasp Little Sister's hands.

"Thank you, Risako. I do appreciate it, and I'd love to come do your 'experiment' with you."

Arm in arm, the two sisters swept out of their bedroom and down the stairs.

"Should I put on an apron?" Ellen asked, glancing down at her birthday dress.

"Nah, I'll just have you sit at the table while I work the test tubes over the stove."

Ellen was perfectly happy to take the role of observer, and she pulled one of the kitchen chairs into a position that would give her a good view. The light was on over the stove, bathing the cooking surface—and the set of plastic test tubes and packets of chemical reagents sitting on the counter between the stove and the sink—in a pool of popcorn-butter-yellow light. Though Mom kept her kitchen scrubbed to a pristine shine, a faint trace of last night's miso soup and pork dumplings lingered in the air. By the sink, Risako had propped the chemistry set's box and the pamphlet of instructions.

"Okay," Risako said. Paper rustled as she unfolded the instructions.

Ellen concentrated on smoothing her skirt across her lap and sitting with her ankles crossed in a ladylike pose. She'd grabbed her black shoes from the closet on the way to the kitchen. As she'd expected, they added just the right touch to her birthday outfit.

"Step one." Plastic test tubes clunked. "Pour contents of 'packet one' into first test tube. Easy enough."

Little Sister ripped the packet open and dumped what appeared to be a great amount of periwinkle blue powder into one of the tubes.

Ellen leaned forward, sniffing as a faint citrusy smell floated towards her. "Careful not to spill over the counter."

"I won't," said Little Sister. Her tongue poked out between her teeth as she—very competently—tipped the last of the powder out of the package. "Step two. Open 'packet two' and pour contents into second test tube."

The second packet contained tiny round red gel capsules. With even more deliberate movements, Little Sister transferred these capsules into the next tube. She didn't spill a single one.

"Very nice, Risako," Ellen said. Praise was something a responsible grown-up gave out, and she had always worked hard to be a responsible big sister.

Risako nodded, but kept her eyes on the instructions. "Step three. Pour test tube one and test tube two into test tube three, alternating so the two reagents mix. Well, why didn't they just have us do that from the packets? Ugh, and they call this science."

"I guess these chemistry sets are meant for kids who don't have as good a handle on, uh, *scientific methods* as you do," said Ellen from her perch on the chair. The wooden seat was maybe crumpling her skirt a little. She wiggled from side to side to keep from developing wrinkles.

Shaking her head, Little Sister dutifully picked up the two test tubes from the rack and prepared to alternately pour them into the third one. Once again, she did not spill a single speck of powder or capsule of gel.

"Alright, done. Step four. Add water. Wow, that's it? This really is elementary level stuff, huh?"

"Risako, *you're* in first grade."

"You know what I mean."

Carefully, Risako carried the third test tube, now full almost to the brim with nicely mixed periwinkle powder and red gel capsules, over to the kitchen sink.

"Here's to science, I guess. But really, happy birthday, Ellen!"

Ellen nodded very gracefully.

Little Sister turned on the faucet. A dribble of water ran into the test tube, and the moment the tube was full, Little Sister pulled it away. She held it out where Ellen could see.

They both stared, waiting.

Water trickled through the layers of reagents like molasses.

Ellen shifted on her chair again. "Is... something supposed to be happening?"

"Shush," said Little Sister. "Give it a moment."

Ellen gave it a moment. She was just about to stand up and fluff out her skirt again when she heard the soft hiss.

"Uh," she said, half standing and half sitting.

The hiss became louder. A thin trail of smoke rose from the

top of the test tube, a weird, moldy purple color. Ellen wrinkled her nose.

And just in time, because the next moment the smoke hit her nostrils with a rancid smell like spoiled eggs.

"Ugh, I'm supposed to *drink* that?" No way! Forget being classy and grown-up, Ellen was not letting that stuff anywhere near her lips, rude or no.

But Little Sister had no chance to be offended, because the concoction was swelling into a purple, blobby mess. In a blink of an eye, the stuff was overflowing the top of the test tube and running over Little Sister's gloved hands.

"Blech!" said Little Sister. As if the purple stuff had burned her, she dropped the test tube. It bounced off the kitchen tile, sending a rapidly puffing spray of purple across the floor.

"Agh, Risako!" Ellen cried, dodging the splatter. She grabbed the back of her chair, intending to climb on top of it. She didn't want to step in that blop and get it all over her pretty clothes.

"Sorry, sorry," said Risako. She pulled her gloves more firmly into place before bending to reach for the dropped tube.

The moment her fingers touched the tube, the blop moaned.

"*What* was that?" Ellen asked. She had one foot on the chair.

"Mmmmrr," said the purple stuff.

"Oh no," said Little Sister.

"Mmmorrrr brrrr aaayyy," said the purple stuff. It swelled again, until its bulk filled the corner of the kitchen between the sisters and the doorway into the rest of the house. Ellen wouldn't be able to get around it now without stepping in it.

If she dared step in strange chemical glop that was now forming what looked suspiciously like a face.

"Risako, what did those instructions say about this chemical solution?" Ellen asked. She found herself abandoning the chair and edging towards Risako. The two of them held hands as the purple goo puffed even more. The edge of it engulfed one leg of Ellen's chair.

"They just said 'add water' and that was it! It didn't say anything about...about... about it making sentient blobs!"

The purple blob turned its now-obvious face towards them and gave a wide, watery grin.

"Mmmooooyyyy Biirrrffdaaayy! Iiiit'sss mah birfdaaaay! Mmmm. Mmmm. Yyyouuu mmmake dinnnnnerrr!"

～

Ellen had gone from princess to prisoner over the course of a single chemical reaction.

Not only was the sentient purple blob too big for her or Little Sister to get around, it was also demanding that they make it a birthday dinner right away.

"Risako," Ellen hissed. "There has to be a way to neutralize the reaction, right?"

"Right, right," Risako said, groping for the chemistry set's instructions in her lab coat pocket. It emerged as a crumpled ball. Risako's hands shook as she uncrumpled it. She scanned the instructions for a moment.

Ellen kept her eyes on the blob. It was opening and closing its mouth, making disgusting smacking sounds and sending its horrible rotten egg breath everywhere.

"Mmmmake biirrrfffayyy dinnnnnnnerr!"

Ellen grabbed Little Sister's arm. "Risako, it's forming a hand now. It's pointing at the refrigerator, Risako!"

"These stupid instructions don't say anything about how to neutralize the experiment," grumbled Little Sister. She crumpled the instructions back into a ball and hurled the ball at the sink. "But this stuff is supposed to be just for little kids. Soap and water ought to do the trick. Come on, Ellen."

Risako marched over to the sink, grabbed the dish rags and bottle of lemon-scented dish soap, and began lathering up.

Ellen eagerly followed. Soap was a much preferable scent to the blob. She tried to be careful of her birthday dress as she joined Risako in lathering, but she realized—with a sinking heart—some sacrifices might need to be made.

"Dinnnnnerr for birfdayy!" shouted the blob behind them. Its voice rattled the walls.

"It's getting angry," Ellen said.

"But the soap's ready! Yah!"

Little Sister, with both hands covered in suds, launched herself at the blob. She pummeled it with fists and feet. The blob roared. Soap and goo flew, mingling lemon and rotten egg scents throughout the kitchen.

Ellen stood at the sink, tossing in more soap when Risako called for it.

"Get 'im, Risako," she shouted. Grown-ups gave encouragement as often as possible. Maybe she wasn't doing the encouragement correctly, though, because moments later Risako came flying back at Ellen, and Ellen had to jump aside to avoid being slammed against the sink.

"Mmm, that was tasty, and oh so good for my form!" said the blob. He sucked in a gulp of air, puffing even larger. His strange, foamy flesh now had a yellowish, soapy tinge. Perhaps even worse was the way his voice had become clearer, less zombie-like. "Now I'm even hungrier! And since it's my birthday—did you know it's my birthday?—you two have to make me whatever food I ask for! If you don't... I just might have to eat *you!*"

The last thing Ellen had expected to do on her birthday was scramble to follow a horrible blob monster's shouted directions. She certainly hadn't expected to hunch over a pot of miso soup, stirring until her arm ached and sweat ran down her face.

She'd slopped the broth on her dress. She didn't care.

Every moment brought a new command from the ravenous blob.

"Soup! Bring the soup, that's a girl. You! Make me some dumplings!"

The blob pointed one of its slimy, dripping fingers imperiously at Little Sister, who stood beside Ellen working the cutting board.

"Poof, you're some dumplings," Risako muttered under her breath.

Ellen swallowed her laughter and stretched to reach the cupboard where the soup bowls were kept. As she rose on her tiptoes, Risako whispered at her.

"Ellen, I'm so sorry. I didn't mean for your present to turn out like this. I truly thought using a premade chemistry set would... well, I at least thought it wouldn't put us in this kind of situation! And your pretty dress got all messed up."

Ellen glanced down and nearly stumbled to see such anguish on her sister's face. Little Sister was scrunching her nose and mouth, working to hold back her sniffles of misery.

"Oh, Risako. It's not your fault. I just hope I haven't been such a horrible Birthday Monster as this guy. I've probably been too demanding, even though I thought I was trying to be grown-up."

Now it was Ellen's turn to contain her tears. Not that she thought she was too old to cry, but with a goopy, ravenous monster ordering them about, she didn't exactly have time to give in to the urge.

Little Sister chopped carrots and green onions with enough

force to break rocks into dust, even using the safety knife Mom insisted on. "No way. You've never been so bossy, even on your worst, big-sister-iest days. Nobody minds a few special requests on your birthday. This guy, he's just a big ol' taker."

Ellen sniffed, wishing she dared to engulf Little Sister in a hug. Instead, she gingerly lifted a soup bowl down from the shelf and ladled a helping of miso soup into it. "There has to be some way to get rid of him. We've gotten out of every mess your experiments have caused so far. Why shouldn't we get out of this one?"

Little Sister sighed. "This one wasn't one of my experiments. I guess I don't know enough about how these chemistry sets work."

A loud boom set everything in the kitchen rattling. Little Sister's safety knife skittered across the cutting board. Ellen's bowl of soup sloshed onto the counter.

"Where's my soup? I'm starrrrving here!"

Ellen plastered on a smile and whirled to face their experiment-turned-captor. "It's coming, just a minute! You asked for dumplings, but my sister needs help to prepare them properly."

"Well, hurry it up, then."

Quickly, Ellen whipped back around and grabbed Risako's arm. She dragged her over to the refrigerator, opened the door, and ducked her head inside as if she were searching for some vital ingredient. Risako ducked her head in, too.

Together, the two of them leaned into the cold air and shifted milk and eggs, slices of fish waiting to be turned into sushi, and squeezy bottles of mayonnaise. The entire middle shelf was taken up by an enormous sheet cake decorated in white frosting and delicate pink and green roses. Ellen's heart gave a tiny lurch at the sight of her birthday cake, the capstone of what was meant to be a perfect night. But she had more important things to worry about right now.

This was the best chance they'd have for a private scheming session, and Ellen had just gotten the spark of an idea.

"You said this wasn't one of your experiments, but maybe that's the problem. We need to make it one by using one of your prototypes to blast this guy."

Little Sister snapped her fingers inches from the bottle of mirin. "Dang! If only I hadn't sent my rocket ship off already. We could have blasted him to Jupiter."

Ellen shook her head. "That still leaves him with the ability to come back." She shuddered at the image of the blob reentering Earth's atmosphere after just enough time in orbit to get *really* angry. "I was thinking more along the lines of your multiplier machine. We could multiply ourselves until there are too many of us for him to fight against, then we can overpower him."

Ellen pumped her fists, full of blob-busting vigor. The motion knocked a plate of cheese over, and she fumbled to catch it before it fell to the floor.

"I'm hungrrryyyyy!" shouted the blob. A wave of his rotten-egg breath set both girls choking.

"So-hoh-horry!" Ellen called through her coughing fit. "We're working as fa-hast as we can."

Little Sister leaned closer, pointing exaggeratedly at a bowl of grapes as if consulting their suitableness for dumplings.

"I like the idea, but I can do you one better. I've recently finished work on a divider application for the multiplier. We can use it on him to break him up into little chunks, and then easily pick him up and get him in the garbage cans. The only problem is, both the multiplier and the divider application are up in our room, and he's blocking the door."

Ellen nodded sagely at the grapes. "One of us needs to distract him so the other can run and get it."

"But how? All he wants is food, and we don't have anything

ready to serve yet besides that one bowl of soup, and that won't last very long."

Ellen glanced back into the clean white interior of the refrigerator. Her gaze fell on her beautiful birthday cake, and her heart grew heavy.

But she took a page out of the blob's book and puffed herself back up. She was eleven whole years old today, a grown-up, unlike this baby blob monster.

"Give him the cake. He won't be able to resist."

Little Sister looked ready to cry again. "Oh, Ellen. Not your cake."

"It'll be okay. Just keep him stuffing his face, and I'll dash upstairs and grab that multiplier!"

Little Sister blinked watery eyes but grabbed the cake box.

"What is thaaaat?" gurgled the blob. His bulby purple eyes bulged at the sight of the white frosting, the pink flowers, the delicate green leaves. "A cake for my biiirthdayyy? Give it!"

The blob's mouth gaped, wafting egg stench over poor Risako, who stepped up with the cake held out before her. Greed sent the blob lurching forward.

Ellen eyed the widening gap between blob and door. She could make it, but she'd definitely smear purplish streaks across her dress.

No time to worry about that now. Little Sister was putting herself in danger as the cake bearer.

Sucking in her tummy, Ellen slipped through the gap and darted up the stairs.

Even with a whole floor between her and the kitchen and with her head buried in the mess she and Little Sister called their closet, she could still hear the disconcerting thumps, gurgles, and calls for more cake happening downstairs. Every now and then she caught the rise and fall of Little Sister's voice as she attempted to soothe their blobby captor.

Ellen dug through the contents of the closet with frantic motions. Heaps of laundry, both cleaned and, uh, *waiting to be cleaned*, blossomed out of every possible space. Among them were long-lost pairs of shoes, a few ancient Halloween costumes, a now-empty aquarium whose doomed occupants had long ago taken a swim down the toilet, the remains of a book report presentation Ellen had done on her favorite manga series, *Neko Hime,* as well as numerous discards from Little Sister's science table. It was a lot to wade through, and most of it was streaked through with musty-smelling dust. It coated Ellen's arms and clogged her nose as she plunged into the pile again and again, hoping that this dive would produce the necessary prototype.

If she couldn't find that multiplier soon, Little Sister might be—

No! She wouldn't think about that. She had to focus on her search. Her memory of the multiplier was hazy at best, possibly because she didn't like remembering moments that had almost gotten her grounded due to glitter crimes. But she forced the memory to resurface. Surely it had to be in here somewhere, especially if Risako had just recently worked on a new addition for it.

Another wet thump sounded from downstairs. Ellen jumped just as she tugged on a pile of unfolded clothes, sending the whole tangle of sleeves and pant legs tumbling around her feet.

But there it was! At least she thought that cut-down shoebox with its knot of pipe cleaners poking out and partially empty glitter spray canister lodged inside was the multiplier. It had a second box taped on top of it now, with a milk bottle cap set on top of that to serve as a dial. Crayon letters read MULTI and DIV at two spots on the new box for the dial to point at.

Ellen snatched it up, narrowly dodging an avalanche of baseball caps and hair bands. One of them sparkled with fake diamonds—a silver tiara that would have suited for Ellen's princess outfit, she noted with a tiny portion of her awareness. The rest of her focus was on getting back downstairs before the blob decided it would have Little Sister for its next course.

The wet sounds were becoming alarming in their frequency and volume. Ellen scampered to the stairs, holding her skirt bunched in one sweaty fist and gripping the multiplier against her chest with her other hand so hard she was sure she was crushing it. But the adrenaline coursing through her now made it impossible for her to loosen that grip.

She all but flew down the stairs in a single leap.

The rotten egg smell hung like a heavy cloud throughout the entire first floor. Ellen's eyes streamed by the time she arrived back at the kitchen door. A sound like a giant, moist pair of lips smacking came from inside.

The blob, oozing about between the refrigerator and the stove, had Little Sister lifted up in it drippy, purple pseudo-hand. The cake box lay on the floor below her dangling feet, empty of all but the last few crumbs of cake and a swipe of creamy frosting. The blob's horrible gaping mouth hung open and ready to be stuffed full of scientist!

For a single, heart-pounding moment, time slowed for Ellen.

Ellen knew without a doubt exactly what she truly wanted, not just for *this* birthday, but for *every* birthday.

She wanted her Little Sister to be there celebrating with her. It didn't matter if Risako spent the day doing experiments or dressing up in princess clothes. It only mattered that they were together.

Anger pulsed through Ellen's veins, and she raised the multiplier machine.

"Get divided, blob!"

Ellen smashed her palm against the dial.

The machine went *ka-plowie*!

The kickback sent Ellen staggering backwards. A cloud of sparkly smoke forced her to lift her arm to her eyes. The smoke filled the kitchen, and a cacophony of coughs poured out.

"Risako!" Ellen called. She couldn't see anything through the sparkles and smoke. Had she managed to hit the blob? Fear spiked in her chest. She hadn't actually made sure the dial was pointing the right way before shooting. She'd barely even aimed.

A glance down at the machine sent the fear rocketing higher. The dial was set to MULTI.

"Oh no... Risako!"

The smoke was clearing, letting Ellen see hazy outlines inside the kitchen. The blob remained as blobby as ever, neither multiplied nor divided. That was a relief, at least. Risako, too, appeared to still be a single Mad Scientist. There was no sign of a doppel-Risako as far as Ellen could see.

But the blob had let go of Risako and had instead turned his attention on the rapidly growing pile at his oozy feet.

Ellen swiped at the last of the smoke. "The cake!"

She'd hit the cake box with the multiplier. The last few crumbs and bits of icing were forming into new cake after new cake.

The blob let out a roar of utter greed and began stuffing his purple face, but even he wasn't keeping up with the rate of cake multiplication. The cakes had spread to cover the whole floor. They pressed up against Ellen's shoes, smearing frosting on the polished black surfaces of her toes.

"Ellen!"

Little Sister was on her feet and scrambling to reach Ellen at the door. Bits of cake clung to her lab coat and hair, sliding slowly down her face as she ran.

The blob monster made a cursory swipe at her, bawling about "caaaake," but Little Sister somersaulted under his goopy hand, and he turned back to easier prey.

Ellen struggled through the spreading cake to grasp Little Sister's hand. Frosting squished between their fingers, but Ellen didn't spare a breath voicing disgust.

"We've got to get outside or we'll suffocate in cake!" she said.

"There's still a path to the side door," said Risako, pointing.

The strip of kitchen tile that would bring them out into the backyard grew narrower by the moment. The smell of the blob's rotten egg breath had been overpowered by the cloying scent of sugar.

"Let's run for it!"

Holding frosting-coated hands, the girls sprinted across the kitchen. Ellen threw herself against the side door, leaving smudges of frosting and sequins against it as she fumbled to get it open.

Cake encroached against their backs.

Finally, the door flew open, and Ellen and Risako tumbled out into the sunshine-drenched backyard, coughing and sputtering as they drew in lungfuls of fresh air.

A wave of cake flowed out after them, mixed in with bulbs of purply goo.

"The blob's still eating!" Ellen shouted.

"He's bound to reach critical cake capacity any moment now, if he doesn't stop," said Little Sister, sounding far more composed than anyone who'd just had a narrow escape from drowning in cake ought to be.

As the girls watched, the tsunami of cake diminished, and the blobby purple mass swelled to take its place. But the surface of the blob looked thin and stretched, like a birthday balloon that's had too much air pumped into it.

"Oh no," Ellen moaned. She took a step backwards, motioning to Little Sister to follow. "I think he's gonna—!"

Ka-boooooom!

A high-pitched ringing filled Ellen's ears. She sat crouched in the grass with her arms curled over her head. The air was *full* of stuff: clouds of periwinkle blue dust, tiny round red gel capsules, puffs of flour, grains of sugar, drops of vanilla extract, and slimy raw eggs—yolk and white together—rained down on her. The smell of burnt sugar wafted from the open side door.

Gradually, the ringing faded, and Ellen could hear Little Sister jabbering away right next to her.

"I think he's burst into his component parts, though I don't see how that can have happened," she was saying. "Are you okay, Ellen?"

Ellen shook her head, but only to get the crumbs and dust out of her hair. "I'm okay. What a mess! Mom will ground us forever if she comes home and sees all this."

"Come on, we'd better get inside and see what's up," said Little Sister.

Ellen let Risako help her to her feet and, warily, followed Risako through the side door. What if the blob was still there? What if he was waiting right inside for them to walk into his awful, drippy, eggy mouth? She didn't think she could handle her birthday ending in such a disgusting way.

But the coast was clear, it seemed. In a manner of speaking, anyway.

"Oh, *gross*," Little Sister said in an entirely impressed tone of voice.

Ellen stepped the rest of the way inside. The blob was gone, but some of his purply, gloppy remains were still around, stuck on the walls, sliding down the front of the oven, dripping over the edge of the sink. The flour and sugar and raw eggs were here, too, making the whole scene into a bakery disaster zone. The burnt sugar scent lingered, sticking in the back of Ellen's throat.

Something else lay in the middle of the kitchen floor, amongst the stinking piles of sludge.

"What is that?" Ellen asked, pointing.

Little Sister trudged right through the piles and picked the thing up with her gloved hands. "It's one cake! I guess he managed to eat all but this one before... well, anyway, you've still got a birthday cake for after dinner tonight, I guess!"

"Blech," Ellen said. She might be happy if she never ate cake again. Still, it wouldn't do for anything else to happen to that cake before dinner tonight. "Better put it back in the fridge, I guess."

"Oh, there's something else here," said Risako, bending again. "My multiplier! The blob must have accidentally triggered it himself somehow."

"Probably while trying to eat it," Ellen said, wiping a glop of frosting off her skirt.

"But the dial is set to DIV now. That must be what caused him to break apart, along with reaching cake capacity. Oooh."

A look of horror came over Little Sister's face.

"What?" asked Ellen.

"It's a good thing I didn't test the divider application on one of us. It doesn't seem to have worked the way I expected it would. Instead of simply making its subject into many smaller versions of itself, it apparently breaks things up into their component parts. Hence the separated reagents and un-baked cake ingredients everywhere."

Ellen wrinkled her nose. "Well, I guess it worked out in our favor this time, at least. But let's get to cleaning up. There's only a little time left before Mom and Dad get home."

Little Sister tapped a finger against her chin. "What if we use the divider application? I bet we can point it at stuff until it breaks apart over and over, and we're left with the component protons and electrons!"

"Nope, not happening," Ellen said. "I've had enough science for one birthday, thanks. We're doing this the old-fashioned way."

She stepped through the mess and knelt at the cabinets under the sink where Mom kept the cleaning supplies. As she handed them out to Risako, Mom's apron caught her eye, hanging by the stove. She considered it for a moment, then glanced down at her dress, covered in various muck, goo, slime, and dust.

She shook her head and got to work.

The kitchen was as sparkling as Ellen had ever seen it before. The sight of it, the lemony-fresh smell, and the remaining cake neatly packed away in the refrigerator went a long way to restoring Ellen's sense of how grown-up she'd become.

Unfortunately, she and Little Sister were both covered head to toe in utter yuck. Worse, they had only moments before Mom and Dad were due back.

"Quick, out into the backyard. We'll have to hose each other down."

A wind must have come through, because the carnage that had been scattered across the lawn was gone. The girls made straight for the spigot and the coiled garden hose at the side of the house.

The rumble of the car pulling into the driveway sounded as the first blast of cold water sprayed over them. Ellen laughed at the shock and the way her once-pristine birthday dress clung to her skin. She knew it looked undignified and childish, but she couldn't help it. After all that blobby, gloopy, cakey mess, an absolute drenching in the late summer afternoon felt like a luxurious royal bath.

She was still laughing as Mom and Dad climbed out of the car, their mouths open at the sight of their daughters dripping in the grass.

"Eriko? Risako? What are you doing? Are you—is that your birthday dress?"

Mom's voice sounded like she didn't believe what she was seeing. Dad had one hand over his mouth the way he did when he didn't want them to think he was laughing at them.

"Sorry, Mom," Ellen gasped through her giggles. "Risako was giving me a birthday present, but it made a little more of a mess than we expected. We cleaned it up, though, don't worry."

"That's very responsible of you, Eri-*chan*, but what about your fancy dinner plans? It's supposed to be your special night. What will you wear now?"

Ellen squeezed water from her dress, and then grinned over at Little Sister. "Even if nobody's dressed like a princess or we eat pizza and cake like little kids, so long as my family is celebrating with me, it'll be the most perfect eleventh birthday ever."

Four

The Safari Photoshoot Mishap

Sitting with her sixth-grader friends in front of the giraffe exhibit, Ellen Sugimori did her best to ignore the growing desire to pull out the Polaroid camera Mom had given her for this field trip. Much as she would like to indulge her new hobby with some photos of the graceful giraffes, Ellen had no doubts about how dorky she looked when she was taking pictures. The boys had already pointed it out once on the bus ride here. She didn't need another reminder.

Not only were all her friends around, but Krista Martin, the prettiest girl in Ellen's class, was sitting on the bench across from her. Ellen couldn't—*wouldn't*—look dorky in front of her. It was bad enough this field trip was an all-school thing, meaning every student from first grade up to sixth grade was here. Little Sister was here, primed and ready to embarrass the heck out of Ellen at a moment's notice with her chatter about "scientific significance" and "field research."

But if Ellen was being honest, sitting here for a moment was nice, even without being able to take any pictures. The shade of the strange savannah trees cut the heat of the sun, and the smooth wood of the bench was cool against Ellen's legs. The breeze flowed well here, too, carrying the stinky animal musk away.

All of which would make for a great romantic scene, if it were just her and Krista sitting together watching the dance-like movements of the giraffes. Too bad all their friends were in the way, each one trying to look way cooler than the last.

Maybe it was for the best. Even though Ellen knew Krista liked her, Ellen still got nervous when she thought about sharing things with Krista. What if Krista thought she was a total dork for liking to read manga like *Neko Hime*—Ellen's favorite manga about a princess who turns into a cat every time she gets embarrassed—or for doing photography?

The sound of Little Sister's voice approaching the group of benches pulled Ellen forcefully from her petty worries with an example of an even worse exposure.

Oh, please don't be coming over here, Ellen wished. That was the last thing she needed.

"Ellen, there you are! I've been looking all over for you," said Little Sister.

Erk, so much for wishes. Her friends winced at the un-coolness of having a younger sibling and turned away. Krista smiled, though, so maybe things were still salvageable.

"Eh, Risako. Aren't you supposed to be staying with your own classmates?" Ellen tried.

Risako stomped the rest of the way over, her big, clonky "safari boots" thumping on the leaf-patterned pathway in the least ignorable way. The pink binoculars hanging around her neck bounced off the front of her khaki shirt, and her multi-pocketed backpack fit snugly against her back with both straps properly looped over her shoulders. Her pith helmet sat cocked far back on her head so she could look Ellen right in the eye.

Ellen stifled a groan. Little Sister couldn't have chosen a more embarrassing outfit if she'd gone into the closet intending to make Ellen look bad. It hadn't been the goal, of course. With Risako, the goal was *always* science.

"Hi, Risako," said Krista. Ellen fought to contain the butterflies that set off in her tummy.

"Oh, hi," Risako said. She was busy pulling a notepad from one of her many pockets. "Ellen, I need you to come on the elephant ride with me."

Ellen was already shaking her head no at the words *I need you to*. By the time *elephant ride* was mentioned, her shaking turned to vigorous wagging. She could not be seen doing anything so silly as riding an elephant, even if it did sound like fun.

"I'm busy over here," she said as Risako began to pout. "Surely one of your chaperones can ride with you?"

"But, Ellen, I need *your* help. You've got the camera, and I need photos for my field research."

"You've got a camera with you?" Krista asked. Ellen barely kept from cringing. Krista's eyes were sparkling, but she was probably just being nice.

"Just a Polaroid. Risako, go ask one of your chaperones to take pictures for you."

"Aw, Ellen. Come on. Observation is one of the most important steps of the scientific method."

Ellen's face burned. The rest of Ellen's friends had all turned away from the utter humiliation happening in this corner of the benches. They were talking about going to get some lemon ices at the snack stand nearby.

"The scientific method can ask an adult to help," she said through clenched teeth.

The worst part of it was, Ellen had boarded the school bus this morning jittery with excitement to show off the Polaroid camera Mom had given her. She'd been dying to tell Krista how Mom had encouraged Ellen's newfound interest in photography, and how she'd described her own adventures as a kid, taking Polaroids and watching as the film developed right before her eyes, just like magic. It might not be as cool or convenient as a cell phone camera, but it felt more alive under her shutter finger.

Mom had called photography "the great truth revealer, even better than a painting for showing what someone really is on the inside." Ellen had sighed in wonder, hoped she could take pictures *that* good, and wished for morning and the field trip to the zoo to get here faster.

And then the boys on the bus had laughed at the big, clunky Polaroid case banging against her chest, asked her if she got good reception on that thing, and struck a bunch of dumb, mocking poses.

She'd shoved the camera away before Krista got on board at the next stop.

Krista got to her feet, bright smile still in place. "I'll go with you, Risako. I love elephants. Ellen, I'd really like it if you took my picture riding one!"

Ellen blinked and had to double-check that her jaw wasn't resting on the grass-strewn pathway. Then she had to take a couple deep breaths to steady her heart's wild beating. Krista was more than just pretty, she was also *so nice*. She made everything seem like a fun time.

Ellen wished she could be as open about the things she liked as that.

Finally, she remembered that Krista had asked her something. "Uh, sure, yeah, I'll take your picture."

"Great! Let's go ride us an elephant."

And that's how Ellen found herself walking towards the elephant enclosure, one hand holding Little Sister's slightly sweaty one, the other hand holding Krista's warm one.

There was no wait for the elephant ride, so the three of them climbed the small scaffold that would allow them to reach the tall back of their elephant and greeted the pony-tailed, colorfully dressed woman zookeeper who was manning the station.

"Well, hey there, looks like someone's heading out on a safari," said the zookeeper in a bright, chipper voice, bending to look Risako in the eye.

"I'm doing field research today," Risako answered, perfectly serious. The zookeeper laughed, but Ellen shuddered. She knew perfectly well how dangerous Risako's research could turn. Risako had a whole slew of prototype machines built from materials like cardboard, tin foil, pipe cleaners, and even glitter. Somehow, they all worked as more than the sum of their arts-and-crafts parts, usually with disastrous results for Ellen and Risako.

Ellen could only hope Risako hadn't brought any works in progress on this field trip. She might actually die of embarrassment if Krista got a glimpse of the weird stuff Little Sister got them into.

Krista nodded sagely and put a hand on Risako's khaki-shirted shoulder. "My girlfriend's sister is a scientist," she explained to the zookeeper. "She wants to study the elephants."

Heat rose in Ellen's cheeks. She braced herself, waiting for the zookeeper to comment on what a dorky girlfriend Ellen made.

"That's wonderful," said the zookeeper. "So long as she's okay with riding between the two of you bigger girls, we should be able to set up a nice little expedition for our budding scientist."

Discreetly, Ellen let out her held breath.

Risako's lips twitched like she was thinking of complaining about this arrangement, but to Ellen's relief, she seemed to decide in favor of accepting what she could get. "So long as I can make notes, and Ellen can take pictures."

"Uh, right," Ellen said. Her face burned again as both Krista and the zookeeper looked at her. Here it came...

"A scientist and a photographer! What a great pair you must make. Well, let's get you on Bella here. She's a real sweetheart, she'll be happy to take you around the paddock for your expedition. Here, take these bags of sweet grass. You can feed her handfuls along the way as a treat."

The zookeeper pushed two canvas bags into Krista's arms, then gestured for the three of them to approach the waiting elephant.

Ellen swept her eyes over their ride's large head. She'd been a little nervous at the idea of riding such a big creature, but one look at Bella's huge brown eyes, happily flapping ears, and smiling mouth under her dainty trunk had that bit of trepidation floating away. They might still look pretty silly sitting atop an elephant, but they wouldn't be in any danger.

Krista clambered into the big leather saddle first, followed by Risako. Once the two of them were settled, Krista giggling as Bella took a few twigs of grass from her hand, Risako flipping through her notepad to a fresh page, Ellen got herself into place at the rear. The saddle and the soft blanket underneath it smelled a little musty, but Bella herself smelled clean, like fresh water running over sun-warmed stone.

Ellen settled behind Risako, her legs straddling Bella's wide back surprisingly comfortably. She was a little disappointed to have to sit with Risako between her and Krista, but this was still okay. And with this little space between them, Ellen would be free to watch Krista glowing with undisguised happiness as they rode.

That bright smile made Ellen bite back a wistful sigh. If only she could indulge herself like that without looking like a complete doofus!

But she had no more time for sighs, wistful or otherwise, as the zookeeper clicked her tongue and Bella started forward at a gentle lumber. The rolling motion of her walk had Ellen catching her breath in restrained wonder. How smoothly such a giant creature could walk! Bella must be giving those giraffes some stiff competition in gracefulness. Ellen's fingers twitched against Risako's khaki shirt, itching to grab her camera.

"This is incredible! Quick, Ellen, get a picture of the movement of her legs, okay?" Risako said. She scribbled furiously in her notepad, leaning far to the side and craning her neck to get a better look at something.

Ellen grabbed Risako's collar and hauled her back into her seat. "Quit that. Now I know why you had to ride in the middle. Please don't make me look bad in front of Krista, okay?" How embarrassing would it be for Little Sister to fall off the elephant before they'd even gotten a few steps away from the station?

"Just take those pictures. I don't want to miss this opportunity to collect data!"

Meanwhile, Bella marched along the trail through the verdant paddock steadily, and Krista's melodious laughter flowed. The sun was warmer out here, heightening the scent of green leaves and flowers growing beside the track.

Krista pointed to a huge tree with a thick, bare trunk and leafy branches on top like a crown. "Look at that baobab tree! This really is just like a safari, isn't it, Ellen?"

Bella was making her way towards that tree, and Ellen knew it would make an amazing background for a photo. She pulled her camera out of her pack, hefting it in her hands. She chewed on her lower lip, uncertain what Krista would think if she snapped a picture right now.

Then Krista turned her smile right at Ellen. "Take my picture, Ellen. Try and get Bella's trunk in the frame, too!"

She held out another fistful of grass from the bags for Bella to take.

Ellen, feeling hypnotized by Krista's bubbly request, lifted the camera to her eye.

Looking at the world through the lens felt nice, like she could see things as more real, somehow. The texture of the baobab tree's bark stood out in stark detail, the grooves in Bella's skin looked softer, and the flowers showed their colors more vividly. Krista was a shining spot right in the middle of everything, and Ellen's focus pulled to her like a magnet.

She waited for her moment... Bella's trunk curled upwards, grass dangling from the end...Little Sister's head ducked out of the way, fiddling with something from her own backpack... Krista's soft, affectionate expression as she scratched Bella's head...

Click!

Ellen lowered the camera, ready to catch the Polaroid from the slot at the bottom. But the Polaroid didn't come out, and instead of finding her companions ready to watch the slow development of the film into the image she'd captured, she re-emerged from her photography flow to an elephant trumpeting in alarm and Krista nowhere to be seen.

"Krista?" Ellen called.

The elephant gave another trumpet, then, to Ellen's horror, leaped forward and ran off of the planned track.

In front of her, Risako gave a cry of distress. "My notes!"

Her notebook fluttered to the dusty ground, lost to their reach as Bella barreled through the scrubby savannah brush, out of the riding paddock, and into the wide grassy expanse of the savannah enclosure.

~

Ellen held onto the straps of the saddle for dear life as Bella continued her one-elephant stampede. In front of her, Risako held on, too. She glanced back at Ellen again and again, her eyes as wide as ramen bowls.

Hot wind tore through Ellen's hair and across her face, barely enough to wick the sweat of fear from her brow.

In between frantic thoughts about impending death by falling from an elephant's back, Ellen wondered over and over what had become of Krista. Had she slipped from Bella's saddle in the fraction of a second between Ellen taking her picture and lowering the camera?

But most of the time, Bella's wild gait and loud trumpeting kept Ellen too distracted to think at all.

She'd managed to hold onto her camera and its jammed Polaroid, somehow. Her backpack was slipping down her arm. Tall grasses whipped at their legs as Bella pounded through them. Clouds of insects swarmed in startled clouds, but Ellen didn't dare lift a hand to wave them away. The combination of grass and bugs screened Ellen's vision beyond Risako's back in front of her.

Suddenly, the grasses parted, and the bugs swirled up and away. A wide, open vista of shorter, golden grass spread before them, dotted with groups of other animals. A slow-moving river lay like a silvery ribbon ahead.

Between the river and Bella, however, stood a herd of black-and-white striped zebras. Bella trumpeted again, and the zebras looked up in alert.

The lead stallion reared in challenge, screaming and flailing his black hooves.

Ellen and Risako screamed, too.

"They look really angry, Bella!" Risako said.

"Bella, slow down!" Ellen cried.

But Bella did not slow down. She trumpeted again, her big brown eyes rolling in fear.

Ellen tried tugging on the saddle straps, wherever she could get her fingers around them.

Bella responded to that, jogging to the side a mere moment before the zebra stallion slashed his hooves down. The whooshing breeze of them slashing right beside Ellen sounded like a swinging sword.

But by now the rest of the zebras had picked up the scent of panic from Bella. They ran beside her, forming a stampede in truth, kicking up so much dust Ellen struggled to breathe. They jostled together, smashing against Bella's sides and bashing Ellen's and Risako's legs painfully.

"We've got to...get...out of here!" Ellen wheezed into Risako's ear.

"There's no way...to stop her," Risako said.

To Ellen's dismay, it was true. Bella refused to answer even to the tugs on the saddle anymore. She was just running.

Running straight for the river ahead.

A zebra whinny to their left broke the cacophony of hoof beats. In immediate response, the zebras dashed to the right, leaving Bella and her passengers unconstrained again. They kicked up even more dust as they went.

Ellen coughed and wiped at her streaming eyes. "Ugh, good riddance, dumb wannabe horses! I never liked zebras anyway."

But before the dust could settle, Ellen felt a prickle of apprehension. The zebras hadn't just decided to ditch their momentary running companions.

Something had chased them off.

"Uh, Ellen? I think there's something in that patch of grass..."

A high-pitched giggle rose from the patch Risako had pointed at. For a heart-clenching moment, Ellen thought it must be Krista, somehow having gotten ahead of them, laughing at how ridiculous Ellen and her sister looked after their harrowing ride.

But that thought was short-lived. The grass rustled, and a scent like wet dog and long-spoiled meat rose from it.

Bella backed up a few steps, and that was when the monsters leapt from their cover, laughing louder than ever and swiping their claws towards the elephant. Their spotted brown fur and horribly hunched shoulders jogged Ellen's memory.

Risako squealed. "Hyenas! I read a book about them last time we went to the library—"

"You can give me a zoology lesson later, Risako!" Ellen said. "Run, Bella!"

She kicked her heels against Bella's sides. Bella, who'd stood frozen in fear, jumped forward, trumpeting nonstop, and barreled straight into the river. The sound was deafening, but it wasn't enough to drown out that horrible, cackling hyena laugh, which followed them as they slogged through the cold water.

"Oh man," Ellen moaned. She hugged her camera to her chest hard enough to leave bruises. Her lungs burned with all the dust she'd inhaled. Even the water running over her lower half as Bella strode across the deepest part of the river didn't help her feel any cleaner. Up close, she could see how the river water was full of grit and dirt and bits of dead grass.

On the one hand, she was glad Krista wasn't here to see her in such a bedraggled state. On the other, where *was* Krista?

Better to focus on things she could fix right now. "Are you okay, Risako?" she said.

"I'm okay, just a little rattled up. Boy, Bella, you sure can run! But I lost my notes. All my field research, gone! We have to go back and look for them."

"We can't go back! Those horrible hyenas are patrolling the riverbank. They'll eat us for sure."

Risako sighed and wrung river water from the bottom of her safari shirt. "I'll have to start all over again."

Ellen tried not to roll her eyes. Better to live to start again than become hyena chow. "Let's just get to the other bank, before a crocodile or hippopotamus comes along to take a bite out of poor Bella."

Then we can figure out what on Earth made Bella run out of the zoo and into the real, wild savannah.

Because that was what had happened. Beyond the fact that the grassy plain was too wide to fit inside the zoo, and the river too long as well, Ellen knew no zoo would keep predators like hyenas penned in with their natural prey.

Besides, this unexpected safari had a distinct, familiar feel to it.

Something had happened, and Ellen had a growing suspicion that the *something* was of a scientific nature.

They didn't run into any crocodiles on their way to the opposite bank of the river, but by the time they got here, Ellen was so rubbery from the adrenaline of the whole ordeal that she more or less slid from Bella's saddle. She landed with a squishy thump in a clump of tall river grass. Her camera bounced out of her grip and tumbled onto a drier patch.

Risako followed her, and though she managed to land on her feet, she also sent a spray of muddy water flying into Ellen's face.

"Sorry!" she said as Ellen spluttered.

"Sorry?" Ellen said, wiping muck from her eyes. "*Sorry? That's all you have to say for yourself here?* I know you've done some experiment that's put us in this horrible predicament! This was supposed to be a nice, fun day at the zoo. I was supposed to be able to hang out with my friends and not have to worry about weird science happening to me. But what do I get? My annoying Little Sister, making a nuisance of herself in front of everyone."

Ellen was breathing hard by the end of her rant. But Little Sister wasn't listening. She wasn't even looking at Ellen. Instead, she was crouched down in the grass, turning Ellen's camera over in her dusty hands.

"Hey!" Ellen said, lurching to her feet. "Don't touch my camera."

"The picture you took is jammed in the slot."

Ellen bit back further anger. Clearly, it wasn't getting through anyway, so there was no point in wasting her energy. "I know. I hope it's not broken."

Risako gave the camera a light shake. "Nah, I don't think so. Here, hand me a little stick or something."

Ellen stared at Risako, barely managing to keep her jaw closed. She wanted to poke around in her camera with a stick? If it wasn't already broken, it sure would be after that sort of treatment! There was no way Ellen was going to hunt down any sort of stick for Risako, no matter wha—

Something tapped Ellen's shoulder.

Ellen jumped, made a sound like a scared puppy yipping, and whirled around to see who had snuck up on her.

Bella the elephant stood there, her trunk curled around a bundle of small twigs. Some of them still dripped with river water. Her big brown eyes shone with what could only be eagerness.

"Oh, uh," Ellen said. That itchy, embarrassed feeling was crawling up her chest and face. She'd probably looked so stupid, jumping like that. How could she have forgotten about Bella?

Risako popped up at Ellen's side. "Thanks!"

She took the handful of twigs from Bella's trunk and sat back down on the grass to sort through her new tool set.

"Once I get this picture out, we can see what sort of data you got with your shot. Drawing conclusions from data is almost as important a step of the scientific method as observation is. Come hold these extra sticks for me, yeah?" she said, as if she expected Ellen to have followed her down to the ground.

But Ellen remained standing, staring into Bella's eyes. Something about them looked familiar, almost human. Bella in turn tapped the dexterous end of her trunk over Ellen's face and shoulders, mussing her hair in the exact playful way kids did on the playground. By the time she wrapped her trunk around Ellen's shoulders in a strange hug, Ellen's suspicion had grown to a near certainty.

She lifted one hand to touch the top of the elephant's trunk and noticed how her fingers shook.

"Krista?" she said. It came out hoarse.

Bella nodded vigorously and nearly sent Ellen toppling into the river again. Luckily, her trunk was strong, and she kept a good grip on Ellen's shoulders.

Ellen's heartbeat roared in her ears. Her vision darkened, but a few furious blinks kept her from fainting.

In a haze of fury and humiliation, she whipped around to shout at Risako. "You turned my girlfriend into an *elephant!*"

At exactly the same moment, Risako succeeded in prying the jammed Polaroid picture from the camera. "Oh my gosh, your girlfriend got zapped inside an *elephant!*"

∽

"Stop yelling at me, Ellen. How many times do I have to say "I didn't do it" before you believe me?"

Ellen stomped in a circle in front of Little Sister. She'd crushed the patch of river grass into the mud, and the tangy, herby scent only seemed to heighten her anger. Nearby, standing just in the shallows of the water, Krista-Bella looked back and forth between Ellen and Risako, worry making her brown eyes bigger.

"You're telling me you came to the zoo today without a single experiment in mind? No prototypes stashed away in your backpack or, or, or tampering with my camera?"

Ellen didn't believe it. Couldn't believe it. Risako was always ruining Ellen's life with her science stuff.

But Risako shook her head yet again. "Nope, not at all. I really wanted to use the zoo trip to gather data the old-fashioned way, with a notepad and some plain ol' pictures."

Ellen fisted her hands in her sweaty hair but managed to stop herself from ripping any of it out. "Then how did this happen? You *must* have done something to my camera when I wasn't looking."

Risako crossed her arms over her bulky safari shirt and tilted her nose into the air. Her pith helmet slipped backwards, and she jerked to catch it before it fell into the mud. "Well, I didn't. I think *you* did something to it yourself because you just wanted to blame me if your day didn't go perfect and you got *embarrassed* in front of your *super cool* friends."

Her face was screwed up in a scowl that was clearly holding back tears.

Ellen's conscience prickled at that, which was annoying. She shoved it down. She was completely allowed to be angry. Her girlfriend had been turned into a gosh dang elephant!

"That doesn't make any sense, Risako. Why would I sabotage myself? And besides, I'm not the one of us who does science at all unless I'm *forced* to."

Risako's eyes quivered with pooling tears, and Ellen's conscience sizzled again. But her heart didn't twist with guilt until Krista-Bella let out a gaspy, sob-like trumpet.

Ellen whirled from glaring at Risako to see Krista-Bella hunching down in the river shallows, hurt etched along her trunk, her flappy ears hanging limp as flags on a still day.

Belatedly, Ellen remembered how she and Krista had been partners in chemistry lab, how Krista genuinely enjoyed doing those experiments and seeing what reactions each process made. They'd decided to become girlfriends after acing the midterm test together.

"Oh, Krista, I didn't mean it like that!" Ellen cried.

But Krista-Bella had already turned away, trumpeting her sorrow as she splashed along the riverbank away from Ellen and Risako.

"Krista!"

Risako jammed her wayward pith helmet down on her head again. "Good job, Ellen. You don't need my help to make yourself look dumb in front of her."

She brushed specks of mud off her shirt, raised her binoculars to her eyes, then turned and marched off into the grasslands.

Ellen felt like she'd missed a step. "Wh-where are you going?"

"Duh. You think I'm going to pass up an opportunity like this? I may have lost my notes thanks to your stupid attempts to look cool, but I'm not gonna let this be a total loss. Y'know, 'cause I just can't help myself with this silly science stuff."

And with that, she walked into a stand of yellow grass taller than her head. It swished closed behind her like a pair of curtains falling on the end of a sad play.

Ellen stood alone in the mud on the riverbank, with nothing but her camera and the Polaroid of Krista dissolving into Bella to keep her company.

~

On the positive side of things, Ellen had found a dry patch of dirt beside the riverbank to sit on while she considered how unfair everything was. She sat with her knees drawn up to her chest and her chin resting on them, staring out over the endless flow of sunlight-sparked water. At some point a herd of gazelle had come silently striding up to the water and were taking cautious sips while eyeing her suspiciously.

Bugs of all sorts buzzed around her face and settled on her arms and legs, but Ellen only gave them a cursory wave to set them flying off again. She didn't have any emotional energy left for her usual revulsion.

She'd hurt Risako's feelings. That had happened before and would probably happen plenty more times in the future. Ellen already knew how to apologize and get back to normal sisterly affection, she just needed a bit of time to cool down before she went looking for Risako.

But she'd never hurt Krista's feelings before.

Since they'd become girlfriends, Ellen had worried about tons of reasons why Krista would decide Ellen wasn't worth staying with, from being too dorky to having such an annoying little sister to having weird taste in food. She'd been so afraid of being found wanting that she'd barely let herself do anything worthwhile in front of Krista.

Ellen had never considered that she might say the wrong thing and drive Krista away.

And the worst part of it was Ellen really had enjoyed that chemistry class, and not just because it had brought her closer to the pretty girl she'd noticed. Chemistry had been fun. Finding things out, solving problems, and getting interesting reactions had been *cool*.

They'd done a segment on photo development, which had sparked Ellen's interest in taking pictures in the first place. Even though her Polaroid did all the developing for her, it was still fun knowing how the process worked as well as being artistic about getting nice-looking shots.

Ellen sighed, which made the nearest gazelle lift her head from the river in alarm. But when Ellen only flipped the Polaroid picture over to look at it again, the gazelle went back to having her drink.

The image showed Krista, a look of extreme happiness on her face, turning misty and flowing into Bella's head. Nothing about the picture gave any hint as to what had made this happen. All it did was make Ellen's heart squeeze again. Where was Krista-Bella now? Was she lost in the savannah? Was she hurt—physically?

Ellen worried about Risako, too. Just because her sister was used to scientific mishaps didn't mean she was immune to danger. Those hyenas were still out there, along with other grasslands predators who would all probably find little girl tasty enough.

Frustration mounted again, and Ellen ground her teeth as she lowered the picture. If only she'd kept ahold of her temper earlier, they could have all worked together to figure this mess out! Instead, she was on her own.

Another bug buzzed up, a big brown dragonfly, and hovered around her face until she waved it away. As if that wave cast a magic spell, her frustration turned to resolve. She might not be the best scientist of the three of them, but she wasn't completely incapable of following the scientific method.

She would figure this out. Both Krista and Risako were counting on her to do it.

The camera lay in the dirt beside her, looking innocent as the sunlight winked off its lens. Ellen scowled at it and picked it up, brushing dust from the case.

"Okay, you. Let's see what shenanigans you've gotten up to."

Step one of the scientific method: Observation.

"I observe that my girlfriend has been zapped into an elephant."

Step two: Ask a question. Ellen glared harder at the camera, imagining herself as a movie policewoman shining the bright light into her shady suspect's eyes.

"Why the heck did you turn my girlfriend into an elephant?"

No, no, that wasn't the right question. Even the gazelles were shaking their heads over that one, sending drops of water flying.

"Right, *how* did you turn my girlfriend into an elephant?"

Step three: Form a hypothesis.

"Well, I thought Little Sister had put one of her weird machines in you, but that wasn't the case. And I've taken pictures with you before and never zapped anyone into any animals also caught in the frame. So maybe... it *is* something I did? Like Risako said. Except I didn't do it on purpose the way she suggested."

Her own hurt feelings tried to whine again, but she ignored them. Risako had only said that because Ellen had hurt her feelings first.

"Whatever. My hypothesis is that I did something to put Krista into Bella. But how do I test that?"

She wracked her brains, trying to remember precisely what

she'd been doing when she'd taken that picture. She recalled the swaying gait of the elephant ride, the warm, dusty scent of flowers on the air, the way the sunlight had shone on Krista's smiling face. Even the memory was enough to stir Ellen's artistic spirit. It had been such a wonderful shot, showing the truth of Krista's freedom in simply enjoying the moment. Once again, Ellen wished she could ever be as open as that, that she could let herself just enjoy the things she liked without worrying what anyone else thought of her.

A glint of sunlight bounced off the camera's lens like a speck of fairy dust.

Maybe that was it? Maybe her wish had come right when she hit the shutter, but instead of giving her what she wanted, it had made a tangled mess of things.

But that didn't sound very scientific. It sounded more like magic, which scared Ellen almost as much as bugs and ghosts did.

Then again, ghosts existed. She and Risako had proved that one fateful Halloween. If ghosts were real, why not magic? After all, what was magic but science humans didn't understand yet?

And Mom had called photography "the great truth revealer," which sounded pretty magical to Ellen.

"Ugggh," she said, letting her forehead rest against her knees. "I don't want to figure out how to do magic. I just want to get my girlfriend out of that elephant and get us all back to the zoo before we get in trouble."

But that wasn't really true. The thing she wanted most of all was to apologize, both to Risako and to Krista. If only she knew where either of them had gone!

She should have followed one or the other instead of sitting here stewing in the sun. Her skin had that itchy, stinging feel of the beginnings of a sunburn. The herd of gazelle had moved on, but apparently not before leaving behind some stinky messes of their own.

Ellen wrinkled her nose.

A splashing sound drew her attention to a leafy acacia tree beside the river. Apparently not all the gazelles had left, because one was prancing around in the shallows, playfully rearing and pawing towards a little gray monkey dangling upside down by its tail from one of the branches. The monkey squeaked, clearly laughing and enjoying the game, whatever it was.

That's cute, Ellen thought. *It would make a good picture.*

As soon as the thought came to her, she realized this was her chance to test her hypothesis. If she took a photo of these two animals while wishing with all her might to be as lighthearted and free as they were, would they merge the way Krista and Bella had?

Her fingers were already wrapped around the camera. She brought the lens to her eye and peered through it, watching the gazelle and monkey continue their game. The colors came through as sharp as a hi-def screen. The textures of their fur, coarse and tan for the gazelle, soft and bluish gray for the monkey, looked so clear she almost felt their fibers under her fingers. Sunlight fell in highlighting pools.

The gazelle reared again, and the monkey swung from its tail, reaching one finger to boop the gazelle's snout.

I wish I could boop Krista's nose without worrying she'll think I'm a total dork!

Click!

The rush of a well-taken photo surged through Ellen, but she made sure to keep her attention on the subjects of her photo this time. Through the lens, she watched as the gazelle's lithe body melted away into shimmering light, then rushed to enter the little monkey's furry head. When she lowered the camera, a different rush overtook her.

The gazelle was gone. The monkey had stilled his swinging and was instead looking from side to side, as if the sight of the river upside down was surprising. He tossed his head as if attempting to jab at something with non-existent horns. When he gave a call, it sounded as if he were trying to imitate a gazelle's bleat.

The Polaroid spewed out from the slot on her camera, and once it developed, it confirmed the truth of what she'd seen.

"I did it!" Ellen cried.

A high-pitched laugh fluttered out from across the river, and her new-won sense of confidence melted under the attentions of onlookers. Instinctively putting the camera behind her back, Ellen looked across the river.

The hyenas were back, prowling along the opposite bank, their coarse canine grins taunting her.

"Hee hee," they said.

Ellen's face grew hot, but she didn't lower her eyes or scuff her toe in the mud.

"Leave me alone," she muttered. "I don't care what you think."

The hyenas kept laughing, but Ellen turned back towards the little monkey. He'd climbed up onto the branch and now sat staring at his own little hands, flexing each finger and giggling in wonder.

"Okay," Ellen said, ignoring how her voice shook. "Time to put you back the way you were."

She raised the camera again, intending to take a picture while making her wish once again. But as her finger pressed the shutter this time, a slightly different thought went through her mind.

I can be as free as the monkey and the gazelle and Krista. I don't want to be embarrassed about the things I like anymore!

Click!

A surprised bleat rang out, cutting off the hyena laughter. When Ellen lowered her camera, she found the gazelle standing back under the tree. The monkey still sat on the branch. He was making faces at the hyenas.

Ellen smiled. She'd done it! She'd scienced her way into the solution. She'd figured out how to fix this misadventure, and she'd even done it without Risako's help.

All she had to do now was find Krista-Bella, and that should only be a matter of following in the direction she'd run along the riverbank. How hard could it be to find an elephant in a wide-open grassland?

Nodding in satisfaction, Ellen tucked her camera under her arm, stuck her tongue out at the hyenas across the river, then turned and walked along Krista-Bella's path. She had an apology to start on.

She'd walked for a long time, until her feet ached and the sun was leaning far towards the western horizon. The grasslands took on a hazy orange tinge in the early dusk. She'd come upon a hillier place in the wide expanse, where the river tumbled gradually down a series of rocky shelves. The sound of it gurgling and rushing roared in Ellen's ears, but not enough to cover the collection of grunts, hoots, whinnies, and other animal sounds coming from atop the pile of rock.

It sounded like she'd finally found *some* animals, anyway. Tired from her walk, she nevertheless tried to pick out the trumpet of an elephant from among the cacophony. After a moment, she shook her head. Better to use her remaining energy scrambling up those rocky ledges than standing here getting sprayed by the waterfall. Besides, it was getting late. If she didn't find Krista-Bella soon, they'd all be in big trouble with the field trip chaperones.

Securing her camera around her neck, she used hands and feet to clamber over the rocks. Her progress went slow, and she sent a lot of loose stones clattering down the slope to splash into the water below. Still, she took her time and steadily rose.

She was concentrating so much on each movement, ensuring she didn't lose her grip and fall, that she didn't notice the wild creature staring down at her until she reached up to grab the final ledge.

"Ack!" she shouted. She withdrew her hand and reeled back. Her balance went wonky, and the sound of the waterfall seemed to grow louder.

"Shh!" said the creature. It snapped out a limb, and strong fingers wrapped around Ellen's wrist. With another *whoosh* of vertigo, Ellen found herself being hauled up to the top of the ledge. Before she could utter another sound, the creature slapped its other hand over her mouth.

"Geez, Ellen, if you want to join my field research, fine. But keep quiet, or you'll scare all the animals away!"

Ellen blinked, and her heart slowed its frantic racing. Risako sat before her, hunched under the cover of a scraggly bush and tree. No wonder Ellen had mistaken her for some creature; her face was streaked with dirt and grass, her pith helmet sat wildly askew on her head with sprigs of some kind of plant stuck in the brim. Her eyes were wide with what Ellen now recognized as the excitement of science being done.

She smelled like she belonged in a zoo. Ellen wrinkled her nose.

Luckily, Risako seemed not to notice. She was too intent on peering through the leaves of this concealing thicket.

Ellen shook the last of her adrenaline-surge away. "Thanks for saving me. And I'm sorry for what I said earlier. I think I figured out what happened with Krista-Bella, though. I... I followed the scientific method."

"Okay, okay, I forgive you, whatever," Risako whispered, shushing her again. "This is an excellent opportunity to gather data on herd behaviors."

Ellen rolled her eyes at this brush-off, then, trying not to make noise, she crept up beside Risako and looked out.

Beyond the screen of leaves, the top of the ledge revealed itself to be a wide plateau, big enough for many groups of animals to gather. A shallow pool had formed, a calm place for the river water to swirl around in for a moment before taking the tumbling path down the rocks. This watering hole was the center of the gathering, letting gazelles, zebras, hippos, and yes, elephants, refresh themselves after the heat of the day. Other animals lounged in the shady patches provided by a smattering of trees like the one Ellen and Risako hid under. Monkeys swung lazily among the trees, birds flittered here and there, and a single, sleepy leopard lay draped along the thickest branch, surveying everything with heavy-lidded eyes.

Ellen watched for a while, transfixed. She loved leopards. They were such beautiful cats, so easy in their striking skin. Her hands itched to raise her camera and snap picture after picture, but she held herself back. She had to conserve her film to help Krista-Bella once she found them.

To that end, she scanned the elephants more intently, hoping to recognize Krista-Bella. Surely she'd still be wearing the saddle they'd ridden in, right? But the elephants, for some reason, were all bunched together closely, as if they were protecting one of their number from something.

She didn't see Krista-Bella anywhere. Instead, she couldn't help but notice another group had joined them, lurking around the edges of the plateau as if looking for weaklings to pick on.

The hyenas.

Ellen bit back a groan. Did those jerks have to turn up everywhere? And sure enough, a ripple of high-pitched laughter soon trickled in, and a monkey went skittering for the cover of the leafy trees, squeaking in dismay.

Risako shifted beside her. "I wish I hadn't lost my notes from this morning. I don't know if the elephants' behavior there is noteworthy or not. Look at how they're standing up to those hyena bullies!"

She pointed, and Ellen looked to see the elephants had changed their formation. They stood in more of a semi-circle now, trunks and tusks out to threaten the hyenas. The hyenas, in turn, simply paced just out of reach as they cackled at the poor elephant huddling in the middle of the semi-circle.

"That's Krista-Bella!" Ellen hissed, grabbing Risako's arm. "Oh no, she looks so sad, Risako. And those stupid hyenas are laughing at her."

Ellen felt sick, her heart sunken all the way into her tummy. She'd done that to Krista with her harsh words. She'd given the hyenas ammunition to pick on Krista with.

She had to fix this.

She rose from her crouch, cracking twigs and sending a shower of leaves down over Risako.

"Krista!"

Risako tugged at Ellen's pants. "What are you doing? You're going to ruin the field research!"

But Ellen shook her off and stepped out into the open. She waved to Krista, ignoring the surprised sounds of the various animals. A few birds took flight. A couple of gazelles bounded away. But most of the animals stuck around, just like kids on the playground who know something is about to go down.

Across the way, Krista-Bella looked up from her hunched position. Her big gray ears hung limp on either side of her face, her trunk was rolled up tight. Her watery brown eyes sought out Ellen, but she continued to shift around so the other elephants blocked her.

Ellen took a deep breath, but her nerves still hummed. She had no way of knowing if Krista would forgive her. Still, she had to try.

"Krista, I'm so sorry. For everything. But I figured out how to put you back in your own body, okay? Come out here where I can see you, and I'll take your picture again."

The elephants rustled as if they were debating whether the hyenas or Ellen posed the biggest threat to their new member. Ellen held her ground and kept her eyes on Krista-Bella.

"Please, Krista. You... you don't have to forgive me. But please give me a chance to fix the mess I made."

A moment passed. The hyenas chuckled snidely, and the elephants bristled at them again, but otherwise all was still on the plateau.

Then, with a mewling little sigh, Krista stepped out of the semi-circle of protection. She reached out with her trunk towards Ellen.

Relief flooded Ellen, and her hands trembled as she lifted her camera. She was going to have a chance. That was all she could ask for.

Peering through the lens, she picked out the details of Krista-Bella's beautiful gray skin, her wide eyes still shimmering with suppressed hope, the twitch of her tail and ears as she began to open herself into the happy, life-loving person Ellen knew.

Ellen wished her wish with all her might. *I wish it were possible for me to enjoy things as easily as Krista does!*

Click!

The camera whirred, then spit out its Polaroid. But Ellen let it flutter to the ground untouched.

Krista remained snapped inside of Bella.

"What?" Ellen said. Hurriedly, she snapped another, then another, all to the same non-result.

The more pictures she took, the more Krista-Bella trembled across the distance from her. Her ears flattened once again, her trunk curled in.

Panic raced through Ellen. She was running out of film, and somehow, her wish magic wasn't working anymore. Slowly, she forced herself to lower the camera and take a deep breath.

A single high peal of laughter pierced the silence.

Krista whirled away, trumpeting her misery, and returned to the cover of her new elephant friends.

The elephants, in turn, huddled tight around her. A few of them turned to glare at Ellen.

Biting her lip, Ellen backed away until she reached the screening safety of the thicket where Risako still sat.

"Good job," Risako muttered. "Now the hyenas think they're president of the watering hole."

Ellen bit back her angry retort. She didn't need to make any more careless remarks.

"Little Sister, I need your help. I thought I understood how this camera worked, but my wish didn't put Krista back in her own body like it did with the gazelle and monkey I tested my hypothesis on earlier."

"Is that what you wished for?"

"What? No, I wished for, um, well, better self-confidence, I guess. That's what I was doing when this whole mess started."

"Being self-confident?" Risako was distracted, scowling out at the hyenas prowling among the herds.

"No, wishing to be."

"Well, that's your problem, right? You already wished for it, you can't wish for it again."

Ellen frowned, considering. Little Sister's hypothesis would make sense, except Ellen had wished for the same thing when she'd done her test earlier, and it had snapped the gazelle and monkey into the same body. Then she'd wished it again, and the two had separated.

Except... was that right? She shook her head and stuck her fingers in her ears, blocking out the hyenas' taunts and straining to remember exactly what she'd thought as she took the picture that had restored the monkey and gazelle.

I can be as free as the monkey and the gazelle and Krista. I don't want to be embarrassed about the things I like anymore!

That was it! She hadn't *wished* to be more self-confident, she'd *declared* that she would be.

Wishing for it again without trying on her own definitely wouldn't make the magic work.

"Thank you, Risako!" Ellen said. In a rush, she was on her feet again, her camera clutched in both hands.

"Uh, you're welcome? Hey, don't startle them all again!"

But Ellen was too busy checking how much film she still had to slow down. Despite all the Polaroids she'd wasted a moment ago, she still had a good stack left to play with.

"Hey," she called, waving at the hyenas. They stopped their tormenting of a pair of meerkats and turned to look at her. The meerkats scampered away.

"That's right, look at me," Ellen said. She raised the camera and snapped a picture of the lounging leopard, letting her joy at getting a good shot show. "Hah, I don't even care if you think I look dorky, because *I'm having fun!*"

She said it firmly, trying to make herself believe it. Her nerves still sang under the sneers of the hyenas. The nearest ones laughed at her, prowling closer.

Ellen swallowed and took a picture of a trio of monkeys. Their wide toothy smiles in the developing Polaroid made her want to smile, too, so she did.

"I'm not embarrassed to like things. It's *cool* that I do

photography, and that my favorite manga is *Neko Hime,* and that I have a girlfriend who I can squeal at the giraffes with, even if our classmates say we're acting like little first-graders."

With each declaration, she snapped another picture. And with each picture, her belief in herself grew. She didn't even notice the hyenas' faltering attempts to make fun of her anymore.

In fact, they'd quit laughing. Instead, they'd pulled away from her to find weaker prey.

Prey like Krista-Bella, who'd emerged from her protectors once again, wonder shining in her eyes at Ellen's display. She didn't notice the hyena creeping up behind her, its gaze fixed on the hanging strap of her saddle.

"Krista, look out!"

But the hyena leapt and caught the strap in its jaws. With a sharp tug, it sent the saddle sliding sideways, until Krista-Bella had to stumble about, ears flapping, trunk flailing, looking utterly ridiculous.

Krista-Bella wailed. The hyenas rolled on the dusty ground, laughing so hard they were practically wheezing.

And Ellen got angry.

"Don't you big, dumb bullies dare treat her like that," she said. "I'll show you just how much we don't care what you think!"

The joys she'd listed before, her skill with photography, her happiness at sharing experiences with Krista, and the way her favorite manga character could turn into a cat, all melted together with her anger into one simple plan.

Ellen flipped her camera around, pointed it at herself, and turned so she'd catch the sleepy leopard in her frame.

Click!

A wave of tingles swept over her, like diving into a pool of cold water. She closed her eyes. When she opened them, she looked out from her perch in the tree. Below her, the hyenas lay giggling.

She stood, shook out her fur, and leapt down among them.

Get away from me and my friends! she roared. Her voice rattled in her throat, a mix of a purr and a scream.

The hyenas scattered, yelping in fear.

That's right, she called after them. *And don't come back. Nobody around here cares what you think, anyway!*

A clomp of hooves, a rustle of tiny paws in grass, and an angry trumpet of a trunk joined her feline roar. The whole of the gathering at the watering hole had come together to thrust out the bullies. Ellen's heart soared in triumph.

Ellen? Said a tentative yet trumpet-y voice behind her.

Ellen spun on her leopard haunches to find Krista standing before her. The triumphant feeling sank back into nerves.

Oh, Krista, I'm so sorry I said those mean things, and on top of ruining your day by snapping you into poor Bella. Ellen bowed her head until her nose brushed the dirt. *I understand if you don't want to be my girlfriend anymore.*

A soft touch between her tufty ears made her look up again. Krista was beaming an elephant smile at her, her ears flapping joyfully.

Of course I still want to be your girlfriend. Ellen, you were so amazing taking all those photos. And the way you sent those hyenas packing! I wish you could have seen yourself. I wish you could see yourself now!

Ellen smiled a feline grin back at Krista and nuzzled her cheek against Krista-Bella's trunk.

Krista's ears sagged a little. *I don't know how we'll get back to our bodies and to the zoo now that you're a leopard, though.*

Ellen glanced at the reddening sky. The sun had edged much closer to the horizon. But though they didn't have much time left, they weren't quite in trouble yet.

Don't worry, she said, nuzzling Krista's trunk again. *I've got this camera magic figured out now.*

She trotted over to where she'd dropped her camera when she's snapped herself into the leopard. It lay on a pile of developing Polaroids. Carefully, she scooped the strap into her mouth and carried it over to Risako.

"That was incredible," Risako said. "I've never heard of so many different animals working together to stop one set of bullies. I wonder if I could publish a paper about a new group behavior. Hey, what?"

Ellen nudged the camera into Little Sister's hands, then pointed her tail back at Krista-Bella.

"Oh, you want me to take your picture? Uh, but, I'm not so good at that stuff, Ellen. I'd just mess it all up, I'm sure."

She fiddled with the angle of her pith helmet and looked away from Ellen.

Ellen rammed her head against Little Sister's chest. *Don't be afraid, silly,* she said. It came out as a rough purr.

"Oof! Okay, okay. I'll do it, don't worry."

While Risako fumbled with the camera, Ellen returned to stand beside Krista-Bella.

Let's strike the coolest pose we can, she said. *Everyone who laughs at it is just jealous they didn't get to have a savannah adventure today.*

Definitely! Krista said.

Ellen bared her teeth and lifted a heavy clawed paw. Krista raised her trunk and spread her ears wide.

"Okay, here we go. Three, two, one!"

Click!

Krista handed another bunch of sweet grass through the fence of the elephant paddock to Bella, who took it with a dainty curl of her trunk. Ellen giggled, snapped a Polaroid, and passed the developing slide over to Risako.

"I can't believe you're just giving me all these amazing shots, Ellen," said Risako, shuffling the new addition into the pile.

Ellen shrugged. "It's my fault you lost your notes. But Mom was right, there's truth in these pictures. You can use these to start building your research paper. Just, you know, put my name in as a contributor. It might be fun to be a part of some new research."

"I will! Both of you will be listed as collaborators. I couldn't have gotten such good data without you two."

Still exclaiming over her photos, Risako wandered off.

For a wonderful moment, it was just Ellen and Krista, enjoying a moment with the sweet Bella while the sun set over the zoo.

Then a loud snicker broke the silence.

"Ha ha, look at these two weirdos. Who feeds the elephants, right?"

"Oh yeah, I think these girls must have gotten lost. Hey, the kindergarteners are supposed to be at the petting zoo, didn't you know?"

Ellen and Krista turned to find a couple of boys from their sixth-grade class standing in the middle of the path, arms crossed, with a pair of sneers on their faces.

"Ellen..." said Krista.

They looked at one another. Krista's eyes were wide, maybe a little uncertain.

Ellen snapped a photo of the two boys.

"Hey!"

Krista leaned over to look at the developing Polaroid.

"Ooh, amazing, Ellen! You really captured what a grade-A doofus looks like!"

Ellen couldn't hold it in anymore. She burst out laughing, clinging to Krista to keep from falling over. Krista laughed, too, until tears streamed from her eyes.

"Ugh, whatever," one of the boys said, and they both stomped off to go bother someone else.

As she and Krista kept laughing together, Ellen knew she'd never, ever feel embarrassed to be herself again, no matter what ridiculous and unexpected adventures befell her.

About the Author

Brigid Collins is a fantasy and science fiction writer living in Nevada. Her fantasy series *The Songbird River Chronicles, Winter's Consort,* and *The Clockwork Kingdom Saga,* as well as her dark fairy tale novella *Thorn and Thimble* are available wherever books are sold. Her short stories have appeared in *Fiction River, Feyland Tales,* and Mercedes Lackey's *Valdemar* anthologies.

Want an extra Sugimori Sisters story? Sign up for her newsletter at www.brigidcollinsbooks.com/newsletter-sign-up/ and get a free copy of *Strength & Chaos, Mischief & Poise: Four Cat Tales,* exclusively available to her subscribers!

Support Brigid on Patreon! Featuring monthly short stories, blog posts, and behind-the-scenes tidbits in a pay-what-you-want structure. Come hang out! patreon.com/BrigidCollins

www.ingramcontent.com/pod-product-compliance
Lightning Source LLC
Chambersburg PA
CBHW031845170626
46807CB00004B/1634